SOMETHING'S WAITING FOR YOU, BAKER D.

SOMETHING'S WAITING FOR YOU, BAKER D.

A Story of Suspense

by Patricia Windsor

Harper & Row, Publishers
Evanston, New York,
San Francisco, London

To Leonard and Freddy,
possible Slynacks

1

He was free, him, Baker D., free as a bird, alone and strobe-bopping supercool, immute and behooveless. Free from the academic grundge of Simpering Simpson's School for Clots and all the rest of the zeronic earth-treaders. Simpson, everyone at school, the neighbors, his orthodontist, even his own mother, were dead. Most of New York City's population had succumbed to the very first nuclear rainbow fall and the rest were affected soon afterward. A handful of survivors, trapped underground on the BMT, were miraculously spared only to perish while trying to cross the Hudson River to New Jersey in a rowboat. They capsized and one swallow of the churn-ing turds was enough to finish them off.

But he, Baker Dilloway, had escaped nurnburn because he was immune. An internal army of unique lymphocytic macrophages had literally devoured any radiation bom-barding his body. His superthymus was growing instead of receding and he might possibly live forever. (He always knew it anyway since he had never been a victim of mumps, measles, chicken pox or any other mundane childhood disease.) Now all he had to do was walk out the door, say goodbye to his crummy apartment building, fare thee well to West 10th Street, so long to NYC for-

1

ever. He had the whole world waiting for him out there, all his, and nothing could harm him.

First thing on the agenda was to run uptown to one of the auto showrooms and pick himself out a nice Buick station wagon. Of course, he'd rather cruise in a Ferrari, but a station wagon was the sensible way to transport gear. After that, a trip to Sam Goody's to stock up on tapes. Maybe he could find a wagon with a tape deck, but anyway it didn't matter, he could load up on batteries for his Sony. He could have a hundred Sonys! Then a stop for food and supplies . . . then . . . MOVE! Pick up a chick. There would be a chick waiting somewhere, another immutant like himself, a superchick with long platinum (natural) hair; no, better make it red, he liked red hair better. He and Red would take off for the Coast, bask in the sun on all those unlittered beaches. Spend time in Malibu, swing down to San Diego, wind up in Mexico. When and if they got tired of loafing, they'd nick a yacht, sail off . . . hey, if they could find somebody to fly, they'd get a private jet, take off for London, Paris, Rome. Eventually end up on some Greek island or in the South Seas; eat breadfruit and coconuts, catch lobsters, drink martinis in the sunset (he'd remember to bring gin). And if they ran out of anything, anything at all, they could replenish their stores anywhere; they had all the merchandise in the world just sitting and waiting. Yeah, they'd start life over again, just he and Red and a few other clean souls. No more shit, no more garbage, the polluters had polluted themselves out of existence. New York would be quiet, dead quiet. Red could drop into Bonwit's, Lord & Taylor, the whole world was going to be her clothes closet. He'd get himself that suede jacket in the window over on Seventh Avenue. He would . . .

"Baker!"

He would stop by the bank and bask in a few million, then tear up the greenbacks and use them to light his cigarettes (he'd remember to stock up on cigarettes). And he'd have to . . .

"Baker? I'm calling you."

He'd . . . oh shit. "Yeah?"

"What are you, deaf or something? Why do I have to call so many times?"

"I was thinking."

"That's your trouble, too much thinking. How about a little action?"

"Yeah okay, what?"

"What? For instance, the garbage you were going to take down two hours ago?"

"Yeah okay, I'm doing it. I'm doing it now."

He dropped the pencil he had been chewing and closed his logbook, but not before he double-checked the latest entry. Slynack activity nil, 1730. It was always slow on Saturday afternoons, a lull before the night attack. He put the logbook in one of the desk drawers, locked the drawer and carefully fitted the garlic-soaked putty around it, filling up the gaps. Then he went to the kitchen where his mother was sitting next to the garbage bag, smoking and sipping a dietetic coffee soda. She was flapping the snap impatiently. Her hair was up in heated rollers because Arnold was coming to dinner.

"While you're downstairs you can get me a pack of cigarettes."

He scooped the change off the table and picked up the big plastic garbage bag.

"And don't be all night. I want you right back upstairs."

"Okay, okay."

"Well hurry up so you can have your supper."

"What's for supper?"

"I don't know yet, you can find something; only don't mess up for a change, I want this kitchen clean."

"What's that?" he asked, pointing to a dish of sloppy looking stuff on the counter top.

"Never mind, that's for us. Beef Stroganoff, you don't like it."

"I'll get a pizza."

"Where, around the corner?"

"They have lousy pizzas, I'll go over to Mongo's."

"All the junkies hang out there, I don't want you going in there."

"I'll get it to take out. They're not contagious, I won't even look at them."

His mother sighed and stubbed her cigarette out in the ashtray. "You must think I'm made of money."

"I'll get a slice."

4

"No, get a whole one. By the time you pay for a slice you could have a whole pizza."

She got up and went to the counter to rummage in the big shoulder bag she used to carry all her makeup and scripts in. It took a while to find her wallet, which was buried under everything.

"Here," she said, handing him a couple of bills. "But try to bring some change, please."

He stuffed the money in his jeans and hoisted the garbage. "I'll be back."

"Take care of yourself."

"Okay, okay."

"Baker, all I ask is you be careful."

"I said okay."

Exasperated by his mother's nagging concern, Baker went into the hall, closing the kitchen door behind him. He stopped by the hall mirror to give himself a quick check-out. A bunch of yellow roses on the table under the mirror got in his way. Men were always sending things like flowers and candy to his mother because she was on television. But these were from Arnold. The creep. Baker parted the blossoms and peered into the glass. His hair looked greasy again, maybe he should wash it. He bit in his lower lip and took a look at the few pimples on his chin. One of them looked about ready for a good squeeze, but he couldn't spare the time right now. He gave his profile the once-over from the right and then the left and stuck his finger on a thorn. Cursing, he went to the apartment door, opened it and slammed it shut again. Carefully, quietly, he crept back through the hall, not making any noise so his mother wouldn't catch him or, worse, think a rapist had got in. His mother was overly concerned with rapists, among other things. He slipped back into his room and went to the window. It took only a few seconds to remove the strips of garlic putty and then he slid the window open and stuck his head out. It looked clear. But that meant nothing. The Slynacks might not show themselves, but you could be sure they were around. He sniffed. Slynacks had a special smell. But all he could smell was the garlic on his hands and the garbage. He climbed out the window and leaned over the fire escape. Five stories down and empty, all the way. If he didn't have the damn garbage sack he could make time. But the fire escape was better than the inside stairs at this time of day, he had to chance it. Whazoom, he plunged. Past the fourth floor, okay. On the third floor Mrs. Silvestri had geraniums and he had to pick his way through the pots. On the second floor Trotta stuck his head out.

"Hey you," Trotta shouted. "Whatta you doing?"

Baker leapt past. Snick, and he was down. He dropped the garbage and jumped to the ground.

"Lousy kids," Trotta said from above, and gave him the sign.

But Baker didn't have time to lose with Trotta. He slithered along the back of the building, keeping close to the wall. The backyards, separated from each other with broken-down fences and chicken wire, seemed quiet except for the muted sounds of six or seven radios and a baby whining. Then somebody turned up the volume on The Grateful Dead. Baker would have liked to stick around to listen for a few minutes, but he had to get out into the street fast. The Slynacks might have cottoned to his ploy, they might already be reassembling to close in on the backyard. He hurried through the dark hole of a back door and slung the garbage bag into one of the cans lining the ground-floor hallway. He could see the front door up ahead. It was closed, for a change. He wished it were wide open so he could make a lunge for escape, but Lil, the landlady, was having one of her periodic fits of precaution. Probably his mother had been telling her the rape and murder stories again.

Steeling himself against the gurshy schluck of a Slynack's paw, his flesh crawling with the dread of it, he made a dash for the door. He kept his nose wary, ready for the smell of Slynacks. But he couldn't smell much except the overpowering pine disinfectant Lil used in the halls.

Now!

Kapock! He crashed into a body. His mind filled with remorse. Stupid jerk, he forgot to check the stairs.

"You," a crackly voice said. "You, don't you say excuse me?"

He opened his eyes and saw Lil. She was holding a mop

and her hair matched the stringy gray mop exactly. Her tall beanpole body was a good runner-up for the mop handle.

"I was in a hurry," he said.

"Always in a hurry, everybody's in a hurry, what for, I'd like to know, what's the big rush, I'd like to know."

She blocked his way. He thought he could hear Slynacks slishing on the floor above.

"If you have a minute you could maybe help me around here. You're a big boy, you could work for a living."

"I have to go," he said. The Slynacks might not attack with Lil there but he didn't want to hang around to find out. On the other hand, he couldn't be rude; his mother was always warning him to be nice or the rent would get raised. He tried to smile politely.

"A lady like me can't do this type of work," she groaned on. "I should have a super. But what can you do, I ask you, where do you find anybody reliable these days, I'd like to know."

He racked his brains for a suitable answer.

"Where's Katz?" was all he could croak.

"Katz? Katz! If I see him in a month of Sundays I'm lucky."

Katz was the big black cat who took care of the oil burner. He wore highly polished rimless glasses and a cravat with his dirty overalls. But Baker once ran into him uptown, in the Columbus Circle IRT, and he was

8

wearing a suit and a tie and carrying an attaché case. He gave Baker a slow, perspicacious wink before disappearing into the crowd. Baker figured he only moonlighted on the oil burner scene.

Inching his way toward the door, Baker tried to appear interested in Lil's relentless complaints.

"Such a rush," she was saying, "always in a rush. An important personage, I know, got big business all the time. What am I supposed to do, I'd like to know. The whole building should fall down on your head."

As Lil brandished the mop, Baker opened the door and was out. He made it. It took a minute to breathe normally again and he sucked in air thankfully even though it was full of exhaust fumes and the smell of burnt coffee beans. He wiped the sweat off his forehead and started across Hudson Street. He was safe now, relatively; the Slynacks wouldn't launch an attack out in the open. Too many people on the streets. They liked halls, stairs, dark places.

He walked along 10th Street, keeping a ready spring in his steps, his arms held slightly away from his body. Natural, not musclebound, cool and light, the way he saw Takashoshi walk, the cat who taught aikido in the East Village. He used to go over and watch the classes when his friend Benny took lessons. He learned a lot from just watching. He was good at picking things up. Just let somebody try and mess with him.

He was sorry Benny had to stop taking lessons and

9

move to Westchester. Very gung ho, Benny's parents, always doing the right and conservatively hip thing. Sold their house on Barrow Street because the Village was degenerating and went to Briarcliff where they already got robbed three times. He could relax with Benny. As much as he could relax with anyone. A loner was what he was, not by choice but by circumstance. Pursued by Slynacks for most of his fifteen years, it was natural that he should feel old before his time. The loneliness of a hunted man. Outwardly, he might appear ordinary but inside he knew where it was at.

Simpering Simpson and his retinue of clots couldn't be expected to understand what it was like so he didn't bother much with the conviviality. He just played along when it was absolutely necessary, giving the usual acceptable jerk answers when he was asked. Sometimes he longed to spill it all out, but he knew it was both useless and dangerous. Nobody would understand. Except maybe somebody like Gorshin. But Gorshin came down from Maine to visit only once in a while and he didn't stay long. Not long enough to really get into a conversation about Slynacks. Gorshin was cool, but you'd have to build up to something like that. Maybe someday he'd have a chance to tell him. Someday, when the heat was off, he'd take off and hitchhike up to Maine. The only trouble was, if he told him and Gorshin didn't understand, if he started giving him the old that's-very-interesting-but-I-wouldn't-worry-about-it shit, well then, Christ, he didn't know what he'd do.

Preferring not to pursue this uneasy line of thought, Baker put it out of his mind. He concentrated instead on his feeling of confidence in the streets, he knew what he was up against with mere people. People! Common Homo sapiens couldn't harm him. He had bigger forces to contend with in the world, earth-treaders were harmless. His mother wasted all her time worrying. Don't go in subways, Baker (she herself always took the bus or a cab), don't hang around where the junkies are. Don't take candy from strangers, don't even take it from your friends unless it's still in its original wrapping. She was always afraid someone was going to slip him some acid. Or hack him to death in a doorway. Christ, he couldn't even go up to Macy's to buy a shirt without her wanting to go with him. It was a goddamn good thing he hadn't turned into a fag!

He walked along Seventh Avenue, looking in the shop windows, stopping to check on the suede jacket to see if maybe the price had been marked down. All the tourists were inside, trying on. He felt a quick hot flash of jealousy in his stomach but it passed. He strolled on. Down toward the honky-tonk atmosphere of Bleecker Street. A few freaked-out souls scrounged for bread but he passed them by. It's no use, brother, he thought, it's all meaningless. One of these days you're going to wake up and the world isn't going to be there anymore.

Before going into Mongo's he stopped to buy his mother's cigarettes and a pack of Lucky Strikes for himself. He lit up and walked cool, swung into the pizzeria, the cigarette hanging on his lip. The place was pretty empty, it was early yet. He ordered a pizza to go and leaned on the counter, sucking the weed like it was a roach. He caught sight of himself in the mirror behind the row of tables. He looked good. Hair not too short, not too long either (he was no freak). Jacket neither clean nor filthy. Just the right number of patches tastefully scattered on his worn-out jeans. He could even flash himself a smile since the orthodontist had taken off the wires and given him some colorless rubber bands. But he noticed the pimple on his chin again and that brought him down. Only momentarily, though. He stuck a finger over it and looked away, through the plate-glass window, watching the passing scene on Bleecker Street. But casually, disinterestedly (he was no tourist).

It didn't take much to put himself in another dimension. One minute he could be looking at Bleecker Street and the next minute he wasn't there anymore. For instance, right now; he was leaning on the bar of one his gambling casinos in Miami, feeling the ripple of his muscles under a silk shirt, flashing his diamond cufflinks and chomping a stogy. He had the town wrapped up, under his thumb. Nobody could touch him. If they tried, he had plenty of boys walking around with violin cases under their arms.

Listen, there was no harm in a little fantasy, he needed it when the Slynacks weighed heavy on his mind. When he was Mr. Big he didn't have all the lousy Slynack trouble and his boys were there to protect him. And he had dames crawling out of the woodwork. He was it. The big man.

"Here you are, sonny," the counterman said, and shoved a hot cardboard pizza box toward him. Baker blinked, scowled, paid for the pizza and got the hell out.

He wasn't exactly looking forward to going home. Never mind the dangerous ascent to the fifth floor and probable encounters with Lil and Trotta, it was Arnold he was thinking about now.

Arnold was a new one and he hated his guts. Not that he ever dug some of the old ones. All these men were always calling up, wanting to take his mother out and she always seemed to pick the creeps. Frisby St. John, for instance, wearing a perpetual tan and winging off to Palm Beach every five seconds. Baker used to meet him in the kitchen in the morning, dunking danish into instant coffee and reeking of after-shave. His mother would say, "Oh, Fris stopped by early on the way to the office." Ha Ha. (Who was that in the shower, Mom?) Luckily, Fris and his mother were basically incompatible since his mother hated the sun and had to wear a hat, sunglasses, a nose guard and twenty pounds of Sea & Ski before she could set foot on any beach. So she turned over a new leaf and Arnold was what she found underneath.

Arnold never stayed for breakfast, he was very moral. He also made helpful suggestions about Baker's table

13

manners, among other things. Saturdays he went to Brooklyn to visit his invalid mother. Saturday nights he came over for dinner. He made a big point of going home to sleep in his own bed, though, and reappeared on Sunday morning, carrying the newspapers, in time for a brunch of bagels and lox. Baker's mother was getting very into Jewish food because of Arnold. It was a novelty for her after Frisby's fervent WASPism.

Before Frisby it was somebody named Clement, who wrote mysteries and smoked a lot of pot but was the unhippest drongo you could ever hope to meet. His mother had lost the battle of trying to get Clement to give up pot. So she gave him up so he wouldn't be a bad influence.

The trouble was she always had to have somebody hanging around, coming for dinner, taking her to the movies. Well, maybe that's what women needed, it was just too bad she didn't pick some better ones. Someone like Gorshin. Now Gorshin he could take.

Still ruminating on his mother's taste in men, Baker stopped next to a wire trash basket, balanced the box on its rim, cranked his hand inside, ripped off a nice big hunk of steaming pizza and crammed it in his mouth. Chewing contentedly, he ambled back toward 10th Street.

Basically, he hoped his mother wouldn't want to get married. He was used to the way things were. On the other hand, there was always the possibility that she

14

would meet some big deal with a lot of bread who would take them away from 10th Street forever. It would be a nice change to have a place with plenty of hot water and no cockroaches.

Baker stopped in his tracks to contemplate this notion more fully. The Big Deal (or perhaps more respectfully called Stepfather) reached into his trousers, pulled out a fat wallet and peeled off a set of crisp greenbacks, which he began stuffing into Baker's pockets, all the while chortling and guffawing good naturedly at the incredible rate Baker seemed to be able to spend money. ("We'll just have to raise your allowance, my son.") For Baker's birthday he would surprise him with a brand-new car waiting downstairs (the doorman eyeing it enviously). Low-slung, powerful, metallic blue, it would have a tape deck and bulletproof windshield, also tear-gas jets operated by an internal switch. When the time came for him to ram his way out of the city, the tear gas would come in handy. It wasn't that he was merciless, just practical. Some are winners, some are losers, whichever way the frog throttles. He and Red would have to get up to Maine quickly to rescue Gorshin. They would stay at Gorshin's farm awhile, resting up, raising chickens and enjoying the simple life until the air cleared. They might even stay there forever, start civilization all over again, like pioneers. Procreate a new world! Baker basked in this vision for a moment until it suddenly occurred to him that Gorshin might require some female companionship himself, especially if they were going to procreate. For one surprised second he found himself considering his mother in the role. He let the idea disintegrate. She wouldn't be happy living off the land. No Helena Rubenstein, no touch-up jobs on her hair. His mother was a victim of the materialistic fantasy box. He couldn't imagine her roughing it for any length of time. She hated camping anyway. It would be more merciful if she didn't survive the end of the world. No, Gorshin would get himself an immutant chick, a friend of Red's maybe.

His mind an endless kaleidoscope of broken bucolic glass, Baker made his way across 10th Street to his building. Cows, chickens and pigs tinkled through the shards of glittering green pastures and golden waving corn. Red, a cream-colored female with enormous breasts, smiled, laughed, glimmered among the shapes of things to come. He almost forgot to check the stairs for Slynacks.

However, he managed to make it to the fifth floor without mishap. It was just as he was getting his key ready at the apartment door that he noticed something wrong. What was it? A cough, a muffled sneeze, maybe only a foot scraping against the stairs above him. Or the snort of a Slynack taking aim? He turned on a pinhead, dropping the pizza, cold-hot with excitement and a kind of dreadful disbelief. There was something up there!

Practically feeling the long green rubbery touch of

Slynack tentacles, he took a tentative step forward and craned his neck upward. The stairs led only to the roof. Usually the roof door was kept locked. Bolted and secured against incoming rapists, burglars, glue sniffers and general mayhem. But a Slynack could change its shape, reduce itself to a mere slimy thread, slurp through any keyhole.

As Baker looked up toward the roof, the light at the top of the stairs went out. But not before he had seen the shape. Dark, big, humanoid. No Slynack ever wore an overcoat.

Cold air wafted down. The culprit had opened the door and escaped. Baker heard the footsteps moving overhead. He shrugged. Only some cat trying doors, flashing the Diner's Club to see if he could rip off a portable TV and get himself a fix. Baker considered going up to relock the roof door. His mother always liked to have the door locked. But frankly, he didn't feel like it just then. Retrieving the fallen pizza, he opened the door to his apartment and quickly slipped inside.

Naturally, his mother was immediately hovering.

"Baker, I was getting worried, what took so long?"

"Nothing. Here's your cigarettes."

"Any change? Baker, you look funny. What's the matter?"

"Nothing."

"Are you sure? Was that you out there in the hall before? I thought I heard something out there."

"Yeah, I was just out in the hall. Now I'm inside. Don't worry about it."

There was no sense in telling his mother about someone on the roof, she'd only get upset and want to walk him downstairs under armed guard for the rest of the weekend.

"I don't mean right now, I mean before you came in, about ten minutes ago. I thought I heard something, like somebody trying the doorknob."

His mother looked pale.

"There's nobody out there now," he said.

"Put the chain on," she said. "Arnold should be here any minute."

She had combed her hair and put on her makeup and for an almost middle-aged chick, his mother wasn't so bad looking. He might even consider her for Gorshin's mate when the New World came. He'd think about it anyway.

"I'll be glad when Arnold gets here," she said, cracking the cellophane on the pack of cigarettes and tapping one out nervously. She went to the kitchen to find a match.

Baker stood near the door for a few minutes longer, listening. He thought he heard the sound of footsteps, furtively coming back down the roof stairs. Did they pause just outside his own door? Putting his mouth right up against the jamb, he gave his imitation growl, German shepherd style.

GGrrrrrrrggggggggghhhhhhhhhhrrrrrgggg, with a few gurgles and a vicious woof thrown in at the end. He waited to hear frightened scrambles from the other side of the door. But nothing.

"Baker! What are you doing? Put the chain on and come away from the door."

A little disappointed, Baker slung the chain. He took his pizza to his room, checked the anti-Slynack fortifications and relocked his window, pulled the heavy curtains across the glass to shut out night and spies, clicked on his TV and finally sprawled on his bed and started eating. The pizza was pretty damn cold.

The picture on the tube started to roll, but although he was staring straight at it, he wasn't really seeing anything. He was thinking about the drabness of his existence, the daily maneuvers to outwit the Slynacks were not exhilarating but dully repetitive.

The doorbell rang and he heard his mother greeting Arnold. They would have a drink and then his mother would sneak in on the way to the kitchen to remind him to come out and say hello to Arnold and be as civilized as was possible, if it was possible.

He wished, for a change, something really exciting would happen.

2

Mary the Hulk stood with her back against the display window of the junk-cum-antique shop and pushed her rose-colored shades back up her nose. It was only six o'clock and she had nothing to do. It had been exciting, for a while, following the creep with the pizza box. But now he had disappeared inside the building across the street and she was getting bored waiting to see if he was coming out again. Still, she might just as well wait around a little longer. If he came out she'd ask him for the time or something and maybe they could go for an espresso. Anything was better than going home.

She waited, her eyes glued to the doorway through which the Pizza Kid had gone, and wondered idly if he lived there. Probably, with his parents. He looked too young to be living on his own and anyway the neighborhood wasn't exactly crashville. The building was a dump, but it had a dingy facade of respectability and a couple of old ladies were sitting outside on the stoop, gossiping. It was getting too cold for stoop-sitting and they were wrapped up in mothy-looking coats and faded scarfs knotted tightly under their chins. In a way, she commiserated with them. Sometimes it was better to sit and watch the garbage go by. You could pretend for a few minutes that you were ever part of it. Every once in a while they stopped talking and stared at her. She didn't care, people looking at her never bothered her. She just kept concentrating on the doorway, keeping her mind calm and receptive, saving up thoughts worth thinking for later on in the night when she'd have plenty of hours to think. But her legs were getting stiff and even her yoga breathing didn't help. She was going to start moving off, when she saw somebody come out of the doorway. A few people had already come and gone since the Pizza Kid went inside, but this person was peculiar. It was the way he was dressed, in an overcoat that hung down past his knees and a big oversized hat clamped down on his head. With his hands stuck in his pockets, the coat collar turned up and the hat brim masking his features, he was like an invisible man, all you saw was the clothes walking. The two old ladies gave him the once-over and started nudging each other. And he didn't seem too happy about them either; he kind of stood there precariously for a few seconds, darting glances up and down the street nervously, and then he took off at a fast trot. Almost without thinking about it, Mary disengaged herself from her slouch and followed.

She could feel the two women burning a hole in her back. They probably thought she was a hooker or something. She let her hips sway from side to side to give them a cheap thrill. Then she snapped up the pace, the guy was really taking off now. He was even taller than she first thought, over six feet and big. That's why she figured it was a man even though she couldn't really see his face. If not, it was a female amazon. Mary followed him like a pro, ready to look nonchalant any second in case he turned around. But he wasn't turning around, he was too intent on where he was going. Maybe she had a live one. For a change. It was unbelievable what mundane lives most people led. She lost track of the times she had followed murderous-looking characters through dark streets only to have them wind up in the delicatessen, ordering salami and pickles. But this one seemed different. The clothes, for one thing, were a disguise, inept but serving their purpose well. And he was in one hell of a hurry. A little out of breath, Mary tried to appear casual as she careened around a corner and tailed him up Greenwich Street.

The street was deserted, but she didn't consider danger worth considering. Tailing people was her mainline monkey, a habit she couldn't shake. It took up most of her time and she frequently had to cut classes because she'd get so fascinated by somebody in the subway on the way to school. Before she knew it, she'd have passed her stop and wound up in Pelham Bay and it could take hours before she got back downtown again. She always got lost in the Bronx. Once upon a time she was Miss Achievement at Music & Art. Now she was Miss Fatcan who didn't give a fart whether she could play Brahms or not. She was through with competing. It was all a big fat relief.

When she was feeling particularly loony, she called herself The Big Eye or Fat Sister Is Watching You, but most of the time she did it as a job, efficiently, without any fantasy crap. People interested her. She wanted to find out all about them. When she found out all there was to know about life's shambles, she was going to India and the Himalayas and forget the rest of the world.

The Overcoat was now cutting across toward the river. She slowed her pace and used the dark warehouse loading platforms as cover. He still wasn't worrying about being followed, yet he still looked furtive. Oh hell, he was probably another lost cause. Suddenly he slowed and Mary dropped back into the nearest doorway. He was turning his head slightly now and she retreated into the shadows.

"Hello, Miss," a quavering voice said. "How's tricks?" The dark doorway was already occupied.

"Really terrific, I made ten already and the evening's still young."

"Oh, that so?" the voice asked, sounding nonplussed.

She chanced a quick look up the street. Overcoat had definitely stopped.

"Would you lend me a buck?" the voice inquired.

"What?" Mary said absently, she was too intent on watching Overcoat.

"I need a loan," the voice said, gaining a gruff confidence.

"Oh yeah," Mary said. "Listen, I'd really like to."

23

"That's what I thought." There was menace in it now.

"There's only one trouble," Mary said. Overcoat was just standing there, doing nothing, just standing on the corner.

"What's that?"

"I never lend money to friends."

Suddenly the Overcoat started waving, signalling, and he was moving again. She left the doorway cautiously.

"You're nuts," the voice said, and chalked her off.

A dark car, moving fast, came up the middle of the street. Overcoat stepped off the curb. The car braked, the wheels screeched, and Overcoat jumped in the door which was hanging open, barely getting his feet off the pavement as the motor accelerated again. Then it was gone. The street was empty. She didn't even have a chance to look at the license plate.

What melodramatic bullshit, Mary thought. She stood there on the corner for a minute, letting her radar cool down. Now what? Back to where the action is because there was nobody to follow around this neighborhood. She crossed the street to avoid the voice in the doorway and started back toward Hudson Street. She felt frustrated. It would have been interesting to see where the car was going in such a hurry, but she was no match for wheels. Sometimes she wished she were invisible so she could go anywhere, get inside cars, apartments, everything. What a gas it would be to find out what people were really thinking and doing when they thought

24

nobody was watching them. Late at night, when she was lying in bed with her usual insomnia, she would imagine herself invisible, making the rounds of the city, listening in on all the hypocrites, looking in all their medicine cabinets. But it wasn't a case of base curiosity for its own sake . . . she could change the world if she were invisible. She could visit the Kremlin, she could hang out in the White House. There would be no more secrets and all their intercontinental ballistic missiles would become redundant, pointless, because Fat Sister would be the spies' spy, a one-woman CIA, completely impartial.

Unfortunately, she didn't happen to know any secret formulas she could swallow, so she had to schlepp around in her body for the time being.

She found herself thinking about the Pizza Kid again as she walked through 10th Street. What was it about the creep that fascinated her? It was stupid because she never wasted her time thinking about dead numbers. They kept her busy while they were there and then she forgot them like they never existed. But maybe she'd go and take a look in his hallway, look at the names on the mailboxes and see if she could guess which one was his. Anyhow, tomorrow was Sunday and she hated Sundays. Pete, her father, would be mucking around the restaurant, wanting her to douse the joint with Lysol and clean out the refrigerators. And Sondra would shag in like she just happened to be passing by MacDougal on her way to 77th Street and bat her false eyelashes and Pete would say, "Hey Mary, mind the store," and go off for a drink that usually lasted five hours.

For the ten millionth time, she wished she were a boy. A man. Men could do what they damn pleased. Never mind this Women's Lib crap, the fact was you still couldn't get around in the world. She'd like to get on some tramp steamer and take off and never come back. Grow a beard and be like Ernest Hemingway or something. Equality was fine but you still couldn't stand up and take a leak anywhere you felt like. And somebody would always be around wanting to rape you or feel you up. You could be as liberated as you wanted but you still got periods.

She slogged along. It would be nice to have a friend. Somebody who knew what was on your mind without your having to explain so much you got sick of what it was you had on your mind in the first place. But she might as well get used to it. She was a loner and there probably wasn't anybody who'd really understand what it was like. Anyway, she didn't mind so much. Being alone had its compensations. You didn't have all the aggravation for one thing.

The two old ladies were no longer sitting in front of the building, and the metal folding chair and box crate they had been using were left abandoned. Mary went into the vestibule and took a look at the mailboxes. Most of the slots had cards under them or slips of paper with names. In her own building, if you wanted your name on your mailbox you had to scratch it into the metal with a screwdriver because the slips of paper were always torn out. Silvestri, Trotta, Ngoni, McCleod, Dilloway, Walbaum . . . it could be any of them. Oh hell. She had better go over to the restaurant and wash dishes.

She didn't bother to get hooked into following anybody on her way to MacDougal Street, she was feeling slightly depressed. Maybe tomorrow she'd come back and see if the Pizza Kid came out again. Maybe tomorrow Sondra wouldn't come to see Pete, maybe tomorrow she'd get a ticket to Zambia, maybe tomorrow the sun wouldn't rise.

And maybe tomorrow something would happen that was more interesting than the usual schlock that lately seemed to be pervading her life.

3

Gorshin sat on his farm in Sawtruck, Maine, and surveyed the scene from great heights. The world and its chaos were far below, purposely left behind. Life on the hill was peaceful, quiet and safe. Or so it had seemed until recently.

The new neighbors were getting on his nerves. And he didn't know why since he never even saw them and they made no noise. Perhaps it was just the fact of their presence, lurking behind the trees, which was annoying. And a little strange.

Gorshin had grown used to being all alone. Not a soul for miles, the farm was isolated and yet convenient to the small village of Sawtruck. But he didn't have to rely on the village because he was pretty much self-sufficient. He grew his own vegetables and some fruit, all organic, had his own generator in case of power failure, and a well-stocked larder. Down in the cellar he even had survival supplies, a hangover from the old days when everybody was building bomb shelters and waiting for the end. The end might still be coming, but people got tired of waiting around for it and Gorshin had bought the supplies cheaply. But he didn't need a bomb shelter. He was self-sufficient for a more practical reason: he didn't trust people.

He wasn't a born misanthrope. For a good part of his life he had been a friendly person. He had been disillusioned at a late age, when a small portion of mankind showed him how rotten the human race could be. In order to protect himself from them and them from themselves, he had disappeared. Now he found being alone had its compensations. He liked it. Or he had until the neighbors moved in.

At first he tried to make the best of it and ignore them. But they gave him the creeps. They stayed inside the house all the time and never seemed to put the lights on at night. But he knew they were there. A battered Volkswagen was parked outside the house and since the evenings had turned cold he had seen a thin spiral of smoke climbing out of the crooked chimney. And there was a certain pervading sense of unease which had begun with the arrival of the Smiths. He knew their name because he passed the mailbox every time he drove into Sawtruck. Smith. It was one of those noncommittal names.

But he made a valiant attempt to forget about them. After all, they certainly weren't really bothering him. They were ideal neighbors, no noise, no parties, no demands. Trying to put them out of his mind, he busied himself with the garden, cleaning things up for the oncoming winter, getting the last of the harvest down to

29

Mrs. Thwaite in the village to have it canned. This was part of his self-sufficiency program, although it was somewhat marred by the fact that Mrs. Thwaite did the work. Maybe next year he would learn how to home-can the stuff himself.

As soon as he thought about "next year" he got an empty feeling in the pit of his stomach. Would there be a next year on the farm? Things had been peaceable too long, maybe things were due for a change. But, avoiding panic, he went on being busy, spending as much time as possible out-of-doors, knowing that during the snow-drifting months ahead he would be in the study, wiling away the short dark days with the book. He had mixed emotions about the book, sometimes thinking he shouldn't be writing it at all. The book was going to tell everything, give the true facts on what had happened to him. It wasn't for publication while he was alive. When he was dead the facts would no longer be dangerous.

In winters past, he had enjoyed the cozy study and its window looking out on the frozen landscape. But now he found himself none too pleased with the prospect. Without leaves on them, the trees would no longer hide the old house next to his farm. He'd see it as a daily reminder that he was no longer alone. With all his big uncurtained windows, the view would be unmerciful. He had never bothered with curtains, but now he considered asking Mrs. Thwaite. He used to like being able to see out, day or night. But now there was a possibility that somebody might just as easily be seeing in.

Whenever it started to get dark, he started to feel nervous. If he tried to read or play the guitar in the living room, he found himself looking over his shoulder all the time. And when he went upstairs to bed, he found himself playing an uneasy and repetitious game. Remembering details. When the neighbors had first arrived, had anything unusual happened? Anything odd? He picked the hours and minutes over, his orderly, scientific mind was relentless.

It had been a nice week, the kind of autumn he loved, leaves turning red and gold on the trees, a fresh breeze blowing big white clouds across the sky. Certainly no feeling of forboding. The old house behind the trees had been there so long it had become invisible. It had been empty for years, long before he bought the farm. At first its proximity had rankled him because he didn't want any neighbors. The real estate salesman had reassured him that nobody in his right mind would want the old place. It had no indoor plumbing, the well was bad, the road was rutted and full of rock. Nevertheless, Gorshin tried to buy it and its small plot of land to prevent any unexpected conjugality. But there had been a problem with the search for title, time dragged on and the red tape unrolled. People in the village told him it was not considered a saleable piece of property. So he forgot about it. He stopped worrying. And for ten years nothing had happened.

And then came that crisp early autumn day when the truck arrived. He had been covering over some bulbs when the sound of a motor startled him. He hadn't been expecting company and turned to see who might be coming up his driveway. The driveway was empty, but through the trees he caught sight of a truck moving toward the old house, grinding its gears on the ruts. Going across the lawn to get a better view, he half-expected that some delivery truck had taken the wrong turn. He was about to go over and offer help when he read the lettering, Overland Van Lines, painted in bold yellow on the truck's side. It stopped and two men got out and began unloading. They were confident as they hoisted packing boxes through the sagging front door. It was no mistake.

At that moment, his phone rang and he was torn between answering and staying to watch, but the phone persisted and he felt suddenly conspicuous. The call was from Mrs. Thwaite who wanted to let him know the summer squash was ready to be picked up. By the time he heard about how nice it had turned out and all about her daughter's new baby and had hung up, the van was rattling furiously back down the rutted road. When it was gone, everything was quiet and deserted again. The house looked the same as before. No sign of people. He waited around, trying not to look nosy. Nothing happened. He went back to his phone and called the real estate agency. Naturally, the original reassuring salesman was no longer with them. But then, ten years was a long time.

"It's all right," they told him. "They're only renting."

"I did offer to buy the place myself," Gorshin said, and had to spell his name three times.

They wanted him to come in and fill out a card so they could show him their listings. He didn't want to see any listings, he explained, just find out about that old house. "I want first refusal on buying it," he said, but they kept telling him to come in and fill out a card.

Exasperated, he went out to look for signs of life again and wondered how much furniture could have been unloaded in twenty minutes. Not much. From what he remembered, the house had a few sticks in it, nothing very serviceable. The place would be full of mildew and mice. He couldn't imagine anybody wanting to live there.

He found he couldn't concentrate anymore on gardening and so he got in the car and drove down to Frank's Country Store. Frank ran the Shell Station and the grocery and his brother-in-law was Sawtruck's postmaster. If anybody knew anything in Sawtruck it was Frank. Gorshin had the car filled up and went in to get a loaf of bread which he didn't need because he got his bread from Mrs. Thwaite who baked whole-grain loaves every week. Buying the bread allowed him to spend some time getting onto the subject of who was renting the old house next to his farm. Frank's wife, however, said it was news to her as she handed him his change and looked miffed that she hadn't heard. But Frank, coming into the shop blinking against the sudden dark and wiping his oily hands on a rag, said he'd heard some "city people" took it. It was evident from his expression that he had no use for city types. It had taken Gorshin five years to get out of the same category.

"They won't last the week," Frank predicted. "We ain't got no hamburgers or movies heyuh, ayuh they won't like it none."

But Frank was wrong, they liked it some all right. They lasted plenty more than a week. The next morning a dented, rusty red Volkswagen was parked in front of the rotting porch. It must have arrived during the night and Gorshin had heard nothing. The wind had been up, blowing loud, but it still seemed somewhat furtive.

Whenever Gorshin went to the service station, he asked if the city people had been in for groceries. "Never set eyes on the buggers," Frank said, obviously annoyed that he was missing something.

And the nightly exercises in remembering got Gorshin nowhere. There was nothing to really put a finger on. His neighbors were recluses and kept the curtains drawn. And it was really none of his business.

Even the behavior of his big old hound dog, Charlie, could reasonably be explained away. Charlie wouldn't go near the fence that divided the two properties from each other anymore. On the surface it might seem peculiar, but there was a good reason for it. A couple of days after the truck had arrived, Charlie walked into a nest of yellowjackets and got a few bad stings in the process. The nest was near the fence and Charlie was giving it a wide berth from now on. Unusually wide, perhaps, but then Charlie was old and probably just being cautious.

In spite of himself, Gorshin found he was double-checking to see if the doors were locked at night, something he hadn't bothered about for years. And he found himself waiting for a sign, some act that would make the whole situation suddenly normal, like a glimpse of the neighbors emptying the garbage. And sometimes he found himself going full circle, ready to end all the theorizing by walking up to the door to see for himself. But he never got there. Was he scared?

He bought himself a pair of expensive binoculars and, feeling sheepish, focused on the house. There were too many trees for him to see anything. He felt guilty. Suppose they saw him spying on them? It wasn't exactly a nice thing to do. But suppose, and he didn't like to, that they were looking through binoculars at him?

Gorshin, he told himself, the past is past and you need a vacation. Go down to the big city and get yourself straightened out. A short visit to society would make him see things in perspective again. The snag was Charlie. He was against travel. He detested cars, and only long-term faithfulness and undying affection could coax him into anything on wheels. After a short trip into Sawtruck, Charlie was laid up for a week and had insomnia. He couldn't subject Charlie to a vacation. And he couldn't leave the poor old dog alone. In previous years he had left Charlie in a kennel, but now even hearing the word gave the dog fits.

The whole situation was getting him down. He didn't feel the farm was the quiet peaceful place it had been. He felt agitated and was getting indigestion. It all reminded him of the past, the bad old days which he thought were behind him.

He didn't like strangers and he had good reason not to. For ten years he had remained anonymous. Oh sure, they knew he was Gorshin who lived on the hill, but nobody knew or cared what Gorshin had been, or had done, before he arrived in Sawtruck. He was accepted now, quite an honor in a place like this. He had remained anonymous, trying to forget.

But when strangers came along, you could be pretty damn sure that your days of anonymity were coming to a close.

4

Getting out of bed was a delicate operation. He had to be careful. Not like the time he got up to go to the john in the middle of the night and set off the alarms by mistake. His mother came rushing in, wearing a fancy robe. She expected to find him axed to death. When she saw he was all right, she went back to bed. Probably because Frisby was in there with her. Otherwise she would have turned on all the lights and given him hell for rigging up more of his booby traps. Anyway, now he made sure everything was switched off before he set foot on the floor. He had a nice battery-operated arrangement all around the bed, up the bedposts and coming down from the ceiling. Gorshin had showed him how to hook things up once when he was visiting. The nice thing about Gorshin was he didn't ask a lot of questions and expect a lot of explanations. He didn't want to know why, how, which, who, the way his mother (and Arnold) did. It was too bad Gorshin couldn't come down to New York more often. But he didn't dig cities. He was a hermit, his mother said. "A reclusive philosopher," she called him.

Baker sat up, disengaged the connections (they were under his pillow and he was a very light sleeper) and got out of bed. It was early yet, his mother would still be sleeping. He went over to the window, unhooked the alarm and shut it. It was getting cold. Lil wouldn't turn on the heat until the very last legal minute. It was the same thing every winter. They were always freezing to death. By the time the steam reached the upper floors of the building, puffing and chugging through the pipes like a locomotive, it was time for Lil to turn down the thermostat until the evening. They always had to light the oven in the kitchen if they didn't want to crystallize during breakfast.

He scrounged around under the bed for some dirty socks, pulled them on and padded to the kitchen, his shoulders hunched with the chill. He moved gingerly, testing his head for twinges of a hangover. But he could usually hold the stuff, always could. It had been a big night last night, closing the deal with the boys from Chicago. He could drink them under the table any day or night. Yeah, the deal had gone good and the syndicate was behind him. Now all he had to do was rub out a few unwanted numbers in New York and everything was go. They wanted him to hire a hit-man, but he would do the job himself. Alone. No witnesses, the best way. He sighed and rubbed the back of his neck. It had to be done.

He went to the refrigerator, got out a can of V-8, cut two quick clean triangles in the top with a church key and drank straight from the can. A little tomato juice for the kidneys. Then he stuck a Lucky Strike in his mouth and lit up. Aaaah, that was better. Holding the can of juice, he went to the window, leaned an arm on the frame and looked down into the airshaft. There were his boys waiting for him down there in the car, ready to take him up to Riverdale to look at the books. He'd have a couple of dry white ones to take the edge off, a nice lunch, some of those T-bones they hoisted, and then pick up the chicks (he always had several girls on call at all times); they'd drive out to the airport where his private jet would be revving up and fly down to Miami for the evening. He had to check on the casinos and he always combined business with pleasure.

He patted the rod in the shoulder holster he always wore (he slept in it). Yeah, it was a lonely life, but in his line of work he couldn't afford a conscience. He belched on the juice and tasted the acrid bitterness of tobacco in his mouth.

"Baker, what the hell are you doing smoking before breakfast?"

His mother came into the kitchen. She was wearing her old robe with the torn sleeve (Arnold was home in his own bed) and Baker could see a pack of cigarettes sticking out of the pocket.

She saw his glance and said, "I never smoked before breakfast in my life."

He threw the half-smoked butt into the sink.

"In the ashtray if you don't mind." She started taking eggs out of the refrigerator.

"I don't want any breakfast," Baker said. His stomach felt slightly queasy.

"Sit down," she said firmly. She put the frying pan on

the stove, lit the burner and knifed in a pat of butter.

"Arnold and I are going out for brunch today," she said. "And then to the park. Would you like to come with us? To the park, I mean; I know you don't enjoy getting dressed up for brunch." But Baker knew she was just preventing a table-manners scene with Arnold. Whenever possible, she fed Arnold and her son separately. She fluctuated between taking Arnold's advice on her son's table manners to heart and getting disgusted with listening to him intone at mealtimes. The problem was solved by never allowing them to sit down at a table together.

"What park?" Baker asked, half-heartedly sniffing the aroma of frying eggs.

"Central Park. You don't think I'm going to sit in Washington Square with the junkies."

"What'll you be doing?"

"Walking around! The exercise will do us all good. It's a nice day."

"No thanks," Baker said. He could just see himself strolling with Arnold and his mother. Arnold would probably want to buy him a balloon.

"We're going to have a nice long walk today, out in the fresh air, if you can call it fresh." She flipped the eggs over. "Exercise is very important. It tones up the muscles, gets the blood going." She was quoting Arnold. Baker knew his mother never got any bursts of desire for healthful exercise on her own. If she didn't have to be at the studio, she preferred to sit around reading or doing her nails and taking baths. She had a pair of barbells that she used to keep her from getting flabby. She'd put a record on and lie on the floor doing sit-ups, or she'd dance around to the music. That was her idea of exercise. In the old days before Arnold, she would suggest they get a pizza and go to a movie together (if Frisby was on one of his sojourns to Palm Beach). But now she pretended that all Arnold's ideas were wonderful and had become a regular health addict.

She wasn't so bad on her own. It was too bad she was always being influenced. She tried to change her personality every time she changed boyfriends. Like when she went to the beach with Fris and got second-degree burns. The beach, Fris? I adore the beach, you won't mind if I wear a wet suit and a mask? You would? Well, okay then, Fris, I'll get some sun for a change, everyone should have a tan like yours. It was demeaning; what she needed was a good dose of Women's Lib. Even he, Baker, a male himself, could see that. But she was hopeless. She still thought, for instance, that she was going to be a movie star. All she had was a job in one of those crummy daytime television serials, but she believed someday she'd be discovered and whisked off to Hollywood. Baker didn't have the heart to discourage her. He always told her she was very good if he happened to be home from school with a cold and had watched the show. But he thought she raised her eyebrows too much and waved her hands around a lot. Still, she looked good on the tube. It was hard to believe it was really his mother.

She served him the fried eggs. Asked if he wanted toast. He didn't want anything, but he figured some toast would make the egg yolks go down. While she was waiting for the bread to pop up she said, "Arnold thought you and he could play a little ball today."

"I didn't know Arnold played ball," Baker said, stuffing egg into his mouth to keep from laughing.

"He'd like to see a little more of you."

"Why?"

"Why? To get to know you, that's why."

"I don't want to."

"Don't want to what, get to know him or play ball?"

Baker was silent. He mopped up the soppy egg yolks with the toast.

"He's only trying to be friendly." She stuck her hand into her pocket to pull out a cigarette and stopped. She put some water on for instant coffee and stuck a piece of bread in the toaster for herself. "Try to meet him halfway."

Baker finished the eggs. What he needed now was a cigarette and a dry martini. Flexing his arms to show off the diamond cufflinks, he said, "Arnold tends to be overly critical."

"Oh, Baker, don't start handing out the bullshit, it's too early in the morning." She poured the water into a cup and stirred viciously. "Why don't you just try to meet Arnold halfway and see what happens?"

42

After she had a sip of coffee and a bite of toast she pulled the cigarette out and lit it. "I thought it might be nice if you did something with a man, that's all. What am I supposed to do? Play ball with you?"

"I don't like Arnold's type of balls," Baker said.

"Baker, I'm going to give you one across the mouth!" his mother yelled, banging the cup and saucer into the sink and running her hands through her hair dramatically (her grandmother had been Italian).

"Okay, okay," Baker said, slightly contrite. "I can't go anyway because I'm going to play touch football with Roger and Sidney."

"Well, why didn't you say so in the first place?"

He carried his plate to the sink as penance and squirted some Joy on it. He rinsed it off and stuck it in the dish drainer and started to inch his way out the door.

"Hey wait a minute," his mother said. "Since when are you seeing Roger and Sidney?" At that moment, the doorbell rang.

His mother, losing all interest in his friends, plunked down her cigarette and screamed, "My god! What time is it? That can't be Arnold already!"

She clutched her robe. "Quick, Baker, see who it is. If it's Arnold, tell him to make himself at home, I'm not ready." She ran off to the bathroom muttering, "Who can it be? At this hour, who?"

Actually, his mother always got very excited when the doorbell rang. She was a little afraid of the doorbell and she preferred the telephone, but on the whole she

43

always answered both with overwhelming optimism. Any caller was potential intrigue. Bells could mean money, contracts, stardom.

Baker picked up the intercom and said, "Who is it?" The intercom, as usual, wasn't working. It had been grudgingly installed by Lil who did it only for the law. Once done, she lost all interest in its upkeep. Baker pressed the buzzer to release the lobby door and unchained and unbolted his own door. He walked out on the landing and shouted down the stairwell, "Who is it?"

There was no answer. No sound or sign of anyone coming up.

Slynacks? It was as unlike them to ring doorbells as it was for Arnold to arrive too early. Baker had a quick sniff and a look up the roof stairs before he fled back into the apartment.

"Well?" his mother asked, poking her head out the bathroom door.

"It was nobody," Baker said.

Disgusted, his mother banged the door shut. Baker went to his room. He got out his logbook and made the morning's entry. Then he felt bored. What was he going to do today if not go up to Central Park with Arnold? Since Benny left, he felt at loose ends. You could always call Benny up and suggest anything and Benny would be glad to do it with you. Usually they just bummed around, went over to Washington Square (he didn't tell his mother), swung on the swings and climbed the monkey bars until they were kicked out by some of the mothers who told them they were too old and why didn't they leave the children's playground for the little kids. Or they'd ride bikes down to the Battery and get on the ferry to Staten Island. Benny had a bike and he let Baker borrow his sister's. Baker didn't like riding a girl's bike so much, but it was better than nothing. He didn't have his own bike, his mother said there was no room to store it and he'd have to carry it up five flights because if he left it downstairs it would get stolen like Mrs. Silvestri's grandson's bike. If he said he didn't mind carrying it up five flights, she said, what did he think, she was made out of money?

Basically, you had to be a voyeur to enjoy New York. The trouble was, he never had a moment's relaxation to indulge himself in watching anything but his own safety. He always had to be on guard. The Slynacks would be getting conditioned to earth by now, they would be thinking about attacking in the open before long. For all he knew, they might even have learned how to change their shape, they might even take the form of human men and women. When that happened, he'd have to triple his precautions. There would be no quick way of knowing about anybody. Suppose some guy stopped him in the street to ask for directions. How could he tell if it was someone on the level or a Slynack?

Baker got goose pimples when he thought of it. But in a way, it inspired him. He wouldn't have time to be bored then. Everyone he came into contact with would be suspect. Human, or extraterrestrial? But if the Slynacks took human form they'd have to get rid of their smell. They'd have to use a lot of deodorant.

So what should he do in the meantime? It was a nice sunny day and it was Sunday and he knew that the Slynacks sometimes tapered off on Sundays, whether out of deference to some religious mania or just because they needed a rest. On Sundays Baker sometimes made the Search.

Somewhere in the city, he didn't know where, was the Slynack stronghold, a subterranean tunnel that could be reached only through an elevator shaft. Baker had been searching for it for a long time. He had copious notes and a detailed map showing which buildings he had already cased. He knew it must be a fairly recent structure, nothing more than, say, ten years old. Because when the Slynacks had first landed on earth, they didn't have much in the way of a headquarters. They dispersed in all directions and a lot of them were destroyed. But they wised up and started looking around for a site. No doubt they worked under cover of night and used the newly laid foundation of some office or apartment building site, taking advantage of the ready-made hole in the ground. What they had done was to dig a secret tunnel which they later connected up with an elevator shaft. Nobody would know the elevator had a secret panel in it, only the Slynacks. This was how they brought their human victims down beneath the surface of the city. Naturally, a Slynack didn't need an elevator, he could squirt himself down any shaft without thinking twice. But the bodies had to be transported. So they'd use the elevator, take it to the basement, open the secret panel and have easy access to their tunnel. Baker knew what they needed the bodies for. It was all part of the big plan. With the bodies of humans the Slynacks could become men.

Slynacks gravitated toward tunnels of any kind, most likely because they were a burrowing people on their own planet. And anyway, they couldn't rent a regular apartment or office for themselves. Tunnels were the answer and also the key. Who knows, there might be whole cities of Slynacks perpetrating in old unused mines everywhere. The earth was probably riddled with them by now. He'd investigated a lot of buildings, but so far he had not found them. It took time and there were problems. With apartment buildings, for instance, there were doormen wanting to know who you were and who you were visiting. But he had his methods for getting around doormen. They could be relied upon to bug off for coffee and leave the entrance unguarded at least once during the day. Occasionally, he'd see some lady with bags of groceries and he'd ask if he could help her bring them upstairs. But usually the ladies didn't want his help. Like his mother, they were too scared of getting raped. Then there were the service doors. Up front were the doormen keeping everybody out, and around back the service doors were hanging wide open. All the brass in front and all the murderers and rapists getting in the back. He'd learned it himself from reading the newspapers.

If there was no doorman, the lobby doors were usually locked. But in most cases, all he had to do was push a bell and someone would buzz the door. If they asked on the intercom what he wanted, he'd say, "Special Delivery." It never failed.

It used to be easy with office buildings. He'd carry a manila envelope and look like a messenger. But offices were closed on weekends and lately they had guards downstairs asking who you wanted to see. There were various methods for this too. Sometimes pure con, like saying he was going up to surprise his Dad. Okay, sonny, it's on the seventh floor. Or he'd give them the tourist bit, Gee I'm in the city for the day, sir, and I wanted to ride in one of those really great elevators of yours. When he had the money, he'd stop at a coffee shop and buy a bag of coffee and danish to take out. He'd tell the guard he was going up to the agency to deliver the coffee. He'd learned the hard way to always have coffee in the bag because sometimes the guards wanted to look. "Hey what's your game, kid? Who are you trying to fool?" He'd have to get the hell out fast.

Yeah, today might be a good day for a search. Maybe everybody would be outside getting the fresh air like Arnold. He could have the elevators to himself. He liked to be sure he was going to be alone when he started banging on panels, searching for the spring. People were afraid when they got into an elevator he was already oc-

48

cupying. Old ladies shrank in the corner clutching their shopping bags. Even some of the men looked nervous. All he'd have to do is say Boo and they'd drop their wallets and beg for mercy.

He got out the folder of notes and started leafing through them. He'd made a lot of reconnaissance trips, checking up on which buildings were likely hideouts. And he kept tabs on all new construction, just in case the Slynacks might decide to change locations. He kept all aspects of the Search top secret. If his mother knew he was riding up and down in elevators she'd have a heart attack.

While he was sorting through his information, the doorbell rang again. This time it was Arnold and his mother was ready. They spent some time talking in the living room and then his mother knocked on his bedroom door. She always knocked because she got hit on the head by one of his booby traps once.

"You're sure you don't want to come with us to the park?" she said, peering in.

"No thanks," Baker said. He got the feeling Arnold was hovering somewhere behind her.

"You wouldn't have to meet us until two."

"No, really, I have other plans."

"What kind of plans?" his mother wanted to know, most likely prodded into asking for details by Arnold who thought anyone under twenty-one should be kept under constant surveillance.

"Like I told you, some of the guys from school."

His mother looked uncertain. She hadn't swallowed the Roger and Sidney story, she knew he didn't fraternize much. When Frisby was around, he had had it easier. Frisby didn't see anything wrong in Baker being a loner. He thought it was a sign of extremely high intelligence and he told his mother so. When she heard that, she made a point to build up the image in Frisby's eyes and Fris ate it up. But Arnold thought differently. To Arnold, kids were not very smart, needed fresh air, exercise and, most of all, supervision. Frisby just wanted Baker out of his hair.

There was a mumble from behind his mother's back and she said to Baker, "Just a minute," and closed the door. Baker went over and listened. Arnold was telling her something. "Listen, Clare [Clare was his mother's name, but when she was in the soap opera she called herself Carla Dill]. Listen, Clare, I just thought, leave the kid alone, he's probably got a girl."

Baker guffawed. His mother opened the door again and banged him in the face.

"Oh!!" she said and looked at him suspiciously. "I just came to say we're leaving now. If you do decide to meet us, we'll be by the statue at Columbus Circle about two. But if you are coming, you better come before two-thirty because that's when we're going to start walking."

"Okay, so long," Baker said.

"Have a good day," Arnold called, jovially. Maybe he even winked.

50

"Don't forget to lock the door," his mother said.

A girl! What the hell did he need with some girl. He had more important things to do in life. When the time came, he and Red would make the scene, but until then he had no time for mere girls. He allowed himself a few moments visualizing cream-colored Red, her long hair cascading down her naked back as she stepped into the pure crystal water of the New World. Baker was right behind her. They plunged, the water swirled. Red swam away with swift strokes and he followed. He caught her under the waterfall, put his arms around her, drew her to him. Her lips were cold, icy cherries (natural, Red never wore lipstick). They warmed as he kissed her passionately. The passion exploded in their ears like the waterfall.

"Baker," she gasped, "not here, not in the water."

"Why not?" he asked gruffly and pulled her to him again.

But anyway, never mind that, there was work to do.

He waited a few minutes to be sure Arnold and his mother were on their way, and then he locked his desk, the windows and the door to his room. He pulled on his Levi's jacket and left the apartment, making sure all the locks were secured on the front door so his mother wouldn't come home and find the rapist hiding behind the shower curtain. He whistled as he went down the stairs. He looked nonchalant, but don't think he wasn't on the lookout with every bone, muscle, nerve and eye of his body. Nothing was going to follow him.

5

Mary had roused herself early, after a sleepless night, and got out of the house before Pete could start giving orders. She went straight over to 10th Street, having made up her mind during the night that she was going to check up on the Pizza Kid again. Sunday was a lousy day and there would be nobody interesting to tail anyway. On Sundays everybody wandered around aimlessly like tourists.

She got to the building too early and unless he was going to get up and go to Mass or something, he was probably still in the sack. Everybody could sleep except Mary. It was okay until two or three A.M. because she still heard all the noise on MacDougal Street and she felt like she was just staying up with everybody else. But by four o'clock the streets would get quiet and, except for an occasional scream, it was like the whole damn world had conked off. But Mary was awake. Pete, her father, slept like a log. When he was home. But home or not at home, it didn't make much difference, Mary wasn't scared of being alone. She wasn't even scared of not sleeping. Insomnia was annoying, not frightening.

She didn't like pills. Pete took her to the doctor once and said, "This kid of mine, she's a regular night owl, the kid don't sleep more than five minutes a week. Give her something, will you?"

The doctor wrote out a prescription and told Mary to come back in a week. She went home and dumped the pills in the toilet. When she went back, alone this time, the doctor looked very serious.

"Now what's troubling you, Mary?" he said. "Do you have a steady boyfriend?"

"I'm not pregnant if that's what you mean," she told him.

"Well," he said, "and how were the pills I gave you? Did they work?"

"I don't like pills," Mary said. "I don't take them. I don't take any kind of pill."

The doctor looked skeptical.

"I don't even take aspirin," Mary said.

"That's silly, everybody takes aspirin."

"Not me."

"You have to take an aspirin," the doctor said, getting agitated. "What if you have a headache?"

"I do my yoga breathing," she said and demonstrated. Hold one nostril, breathe in, hold both nostrils, open the other nostril, let the air out. He didn't like it.

"Buy some aspirin," he said. "You can get it in any drugstore."

Mary got bored waiting around next to the junk shop so she went over to the building and rang a few bells. She thought maybe if she rang the right one the Pizza Kid would come down.

"What do you want," he'd ask her and she'd say, "Nothing, I just like to ring bells."

But nobody came down except an old lady in a dirty housecoat and slippers who told her to get the hell out of the hallway or she'd call the cops. She managed to ring only three. There was no way of knowing if one was his. She went back to the junk shop and waited.

Finally, some people started coming out. They must be waking up, Mary thought, and she knew Pete would be awake, yelling at the top of his lungs, "Hey, Mary, come on it's time to go to the store," and she wouldn't be there and he'd get mad.

"Hey, Mary," he told her all the time, "you got brains, not like your father, you're going places." "Scholarships," he told all the relatives, "my kid's got scholarships coming out of her ears." Or sometimes he'd say "up the ass," if he thought she wasn't listening. Well, she was going to disappoint him. The scholarship days were over. What she'd really like was a scholarship to take care of lepers or something. Something worthwhile.

A man and woman came out of the building together. The woman had blonde hair hanging down to her shoulders and dark glasses on. She looked like she thought she was a movie star and she was very thin. Thin women always looked like they had some special secret going for them. The whole world was on a thin kick and looked at her, Mary the Hulk, as if she were a criminal. A lot of the girls in school always wanted to give her advice on diets and self-control. They spent their whole time talking about diets and being noble about not eating what they really were dying to eat in the first place. Read any book, look at any movie and if they wanted to portray some unattractive schlepp, you could be sure they made her fat. If you're fat then it goes without saying you must be ugly or stupid. Read any of those dumb teen-age advice columns and you found out the prime motivation in life was to attract men and the only way you could hope to attract them was to be thin. The way they talked, all the fat people in the world were deprived of happiness. Anyway, the thin lady walked off with the man who had a small pot belly.

About ten minutes later the Pizza Kid appeared.

He was all dressed in gear and looked like a real fruit. He swaggered when he walked like he'd seen too many commercials.

Mary walked after him. It was easy, he never looked back.

But after a while, things seemed to get weird. He backtracked, He circled on himself. He kept crossing and recrossing the streets. He didn't like doorways and he gave them a wide berth. It was almost as if he knew she was following him and he was trying to lose her. But that seemed impossible. For one thing, he didn't even know her, and there were lots of other people walking behind him, even fat ones. For another thing, he never turned around so how could he know she was there in the first place? It crossed her mind that maybe he thought someone else was following him, someone he knew would be likely to. But then she thought he must just be paranoid.

He finally went down into the subway on Sixth Avenue. He walked all the way down to the F-train platform and waited. Mary hung around by the candy machine, pretending to be looking at the dilapidated candy bars, but she was keeping a sharp eye on him. The train pulled in. He went to the door at the end of the car and Mary joined a group jostling at the center. Somebody next to her seemed to be jostling more than usual, however. She gave him a quick one in the ribs, but he didn't give up. "Outta my way," he said, although there was certainly plenty of room for everybody to get in. She almost felt he was trying to prevent her from getting on the train.

She saw the Pizza Kid go into the car and then she saw him come out again. The jostler, by this time, was already inside. But with a ferocious leap, he came out again. And there was no doubt about it, he had his eyes on the Pizza Kid. The doors were closing and now he was trying to shove Mary inside the car.

"Make up your mind," she told him. "Get lost," he told her back, and he leered at her with dark threatening eyes that left the Kid for only a second before they were back watching him again.

She made out like she was staying on the train. At the last possible moment, she threw herself out the door. She didn't have much trouble momentarily wedging them open.

The Pizza Kid was going up the stairs. The jostler was

56

following. Neither one looked back. The train roared out of the station and the platform was suddenly lonely. Mary turned and ran up the opposite staircase and caught a glimpse of the Kid on the next level, hurrying toward the upper platform. The jostler came crawling up after him and his eyes blazed when he saw Mary again. She stuck out her tongue and kept climbing. When she put her mind to it, she got up steam. The upper platform was crowded with people loitering or waiting for the A train. The Pizza Kid was quickening his pace. He had a neat style, the way he threaded his way through the throng. She silently cheered him on as the jostler dropped behind. In a moment, she was neck and neck with the Kid.

"Hey," she said, panting only slightly, "wait up, will you?"

He stopped for only a second, saying, "Huh?" and then kept on going.

"Hey, I got something important to tell you."

"Yeah?" he said, looking fierce, but she could see it was an act.

"Yeah. Something you ought to know."

"Get lost," he said.

"Don't tell me to get lost," she said, she had had enough of that for one day. She looked back and saw the jostler had got entangled with a couple of mothers and babies in strollers. He looked very desperate.

"I want to tell you something important," she said.

57

They were running up the stairs to the street now. The jostler was far behind.

"Quick," she said, grabbing the Kid's arm and dragging him across Sixth Avenue against the traffic. A couple of taxis yelled obscenities.

Before he knew what was happening, she had pulled him back down the subway stairs on the other side of the street. His skinniness was no match for her muscles.

"Christ, I almost got killed," he said.

"You said it." She checked to see if the jostler was anywhere in sight.

"We lost him," she said.

He stopped. "Who?"

"That's what I wanted to tell you." She took a deep breath. "Somebody's following you," she said, "and it isn't me."

She never expected such a reaction. He went white. White as a sheet she thought, who would have believed it? She hoped he wouldn't faint. He was suddenly all shaky, but he was making a big effort to control himself. "Get lost," he said again.

"I'm serious. He followed you on the train and when you got off he got off too. He damn near broke my leg in the process." That wasn't true but so what.

"That's a lie."

"What? Oh, listen, it's true, he was following you all right, no mistake. But he's gone. Probably some pervert, you know. Let's have a cup of coffee or something, okay?"

The Pizza Kid was still looking as if he were going to crumble. What was wrong with him? You'd think he'd never run into a pervert.

"Come on," she said. "I'll pay for the coffee." But he didn't move.

"It's okay now, what are you so worried about? People are always following you, it happens all the time."

"What?" he gasped. His eyes were bugging out.

"I meant in general. People are always following people for one reason or another. Hey, what are you, some kind of tourist? Have you lived here long?"

"Sure," he replied in a daze. "Yeah, all my life. What did they look like?"

"Not they, it was a he."

"It?" the Kid asked, uncertainly.

"Him, you know, a man, a creep, what's the difference."

"A man," the Kid said slowly. "A man, already."

She didn't know what he was talking about, but she figured he was more afraid of perverts than he cared to admit. "Listen," she said comfortingly, "put it out of your mind. You can't let these things get to you or you won't survive." She yanked his arm. He was like molasses, he stretched. She pulled him back into the daylight. "It's a simple fact of life in New York," she told him. "You have to make the best of it. Psych them out before they psych you."

He looked up and down the street like he expected to see a ghost.

My god, what a fruit, she thought; he's scared stiff. If he ever found out she had been following him too, he'd probably have a fit and die right there. "Come on, you need a cup of coffee," she told him.

They crossed the street, waiting for the light this time, and he kept on muttering to himself about men. "Men, already," he said, shaking his head. When they got to the coffee shop he turned and looked at her like he was aware of her for the first time.

"Who are you?" he asked, teetering on the threshold, blinking his eyes. "Miss America," she said and shoved him inside.

6

"Who's she?" Abraham thought, and he made a mental note to check with the boss to ask if he should get rid of her.

7

It was a funny thing about the dog. He didn't want to go out at all. The run-in with the yellowjackets should have been forgotten by now. But except for a quick turn in the morning and evening, Charlie wanted no part of the outdoors. If Gorshin coaxed, cajoled and bodily pushed him, Charlie would keep sniffing along the ground like he'd bagged a rabbit. Now, Charlie was never a bird dog, or a rabbit dog for that matter. In fact, he liked rabbits. And he used to like a nice walk. He used to enjoy chasing the wind. But now he stayed in the kitchen on his blanket. And all night long Gorshin kept hearing locomotives.

"We're going crackers," he told Charlie in the morning. "The two of us. We've been alone too long."

But before he could start getting soggy, he put the coffeepot on and did a few sit-ups. Then he did all the things he usually did, but he kept on feeling uneasy. He tried working around the yard. The sun was shining and the day was great, but the memory of those locomotives kept haunting him. Not exactly a sound, more a vibration. A dream? Or something real? He looked over at the old house. Everything was quiet, shuttered, as desolate as usual. Giving up, he went inside to his study and tried to work in there. But what was the use? He shut the drawers and straightened out the stack of papers on the blotter. He pushed the chair into the kneehole and closed the door.

"Come on, Charlie," he said. "We're going for a long walk." Charlie waved his tail none too enthusiastically from his blanket in the corner of the kitchen. He kept his eyes shut.

"Don't be nervous now," Gorshin coaxed him. "A nice walk in the woods like we used to take." Charlie opened one eye and turned it toward the ceiling.

"What about it, Charlie?" Gorshin asked. "Come on."

Slowly, the dog got to his feet. He yawned and nuzzled Gorshin's legs and looked up at him imploringly. But Gorshin was having none of it. He led him to the back door. Charlie looked longingly toward his blanket. He groaned and moaned, but Gorshin gave him a deaf ear.

Surprisingly enough, once they were well away from the house, Charlie perked up. He gave Gorshin a smile and was more like his old self again. Gorshin decided to take a real walk into the hills. He was going to put locomotives out of his mind for the afternoon.

They came back as the sun was lowering. And Charlie's head lowered like the sun as they neared the house once more. But Gorshin thought the dog was probably tired out. Gorshin felt good, much better than he had in a long time.

63

"That's what we needed, Charlie old boy," he said as he opened the door. He felt slightly ridiculous having to get a key out to unlock it. What the hell had been eating him? All that nonsense about the new neighbors. He had let it get to him and good. They were probably nice people who kept to themselves. He ought to be thankful, he couldn't have asked for anything better, except of course no neighbors at all; but if he had to have somebody living over there then it was a blessing they were so quiet and unobtrusive. On this note, Gorshin went into his study to find his pipe.

Like a lead balloon, it all came back.

Not that anything really looked disturbed. More of a feeling. The drawer there in the desk, had he left it slightly open? The stack of papers, were they a bit ruffled now? The chair was pulled away. And a funny smell, he couldn't quite put his nose on it. But definitely a smell. Different. He felt the skin on the back of his neck start to crawl. Had somebody been inside the house while they were away in the hills?

He quickly checked the front door and the windows. Nothing seemed amiss. The locks were intact and there didn't seem to be signs of forcing. They were heavy cylinder locks and a plastic card would not have worked on them. He bent down and squinted at the brass, searching for scratches. It was useless, he had no way of telling if the slight marks on the doors were old or new. They looked old. But he was no expert. The windows all had screens on them to keep out the bugs. Supposedly, they couldn't be opened from the outside, a feature that had never affected Gorshin one way or another until now. He went outside and tried. At least he couldn't open them. None of the screens had been cut.

He didn't suppose anybody had come down the chimney, but he looked anyway. The damper was still closed. There was no soot. The fire screen was in place.

He walked through all the rooms, checking odds and ends. There was nothing of real value, just old books, outdated hi-fi records, a broken-down clock that claimed antiquity but was still sitting on the mantel. His money was still in the top drawer of the kitchen cabinet. He had only a small amount of cash, Frank always took checks. There was a sign hanging in Frank's store that said, "No checks cashed thank you," but he obliged Gorshin because he knew him long enough. He checked through the desk in the study. Nothing was missing, but he now felt very definitely someone had rifled his papers.

Finally, he made Charlie come into the study and have a sniff around. Charlie looked doleful and like he wished he never got mixed up in it. "What do you think?" Gorshin asked him. But the smell was already fading. Charlie went back to the kitchen and covered his nose.

They ate their dinner in the kitchen, in silence. Neither of them felt like talking. Gorshin kept reviewing all the locked-room mysteries he had read. But there were no dead bodies here. Whoever had come had not found what he wanted. Could have had a key. Didn't seem likely, but it was always possible. Keys could be made. What about all that business with wax impressions? He supposed it was the answer. Tonight, before he went to bed, he'd throw the bolts just to be on the safe side. He'd lock all the windows too. He couldn't help feeling that he himself was what the intruder might be after.

He cleared the table and washed the dishes, and suddenly he felt like talking to somebody more than he ever had in the past ten years. He thought of Frank. But he couldn't ask Frank to drop by, just as Frank never asked him to drop by. Frank would think it was pretty damn funny being asked. He thought of Mrs. Thwaite, but somehow that seemed even funnier. He could call somebody just to pass the time. He went to the telephone and stood there for five minutes trying to think of somebody to call.

Then he dialed information and asked for a number, probably a new listing, for Smith on Old Tavern Road.

"How are you spelling that?" the operator asked.

He spelled it.

"Do you have a first initial?"

No, he didn't. But how many Smiths lived on Old Tavern Road?

"I don't find a listing," she said. He hung up.

Then he dialled again. "If the phone was unlisted," he asked, "would you know?"

"I wouldn't be able to give you the number if it was unlisted," she said.

He understood that, he just wanted to know. She checked again. There was no phone for Smith on Old Tavern Road.

He went into the living room which usually seemed so cozy and warm but which now had a lot of black forboding windows staring at him like eyes. He felt vulnerable. He got his book and went upstairs, promising himself he would ask Mrs. Thwaite about curtains.

The book was dull enough to keep him fantasizing. Maybe there's nobody there, he suddenly thought. Or maybe somebody was there and they had an accident, a heart attack, they might be lying dead and no one would know. Maybe whoever had broken in had nothing to do with the neighbors at all. Suddenly the thought of dead neighbors became more terrifying than live ones. He was all alone. Nobody would help him because nobody would know.

Unable to stay in bed, he went back downstairs and made the rounds. He slid the big old iron bolts into place on the front and back doors. He closed all the windows and locked them. He said goodnight to Charlie, who was huddled on his blanket in the kitchen. He considered asking Charlie to join him upstairs, but he felt it would be too much for the dog's nerves. Charlie had always slept in the kitchen. A change would upset him, especially now.

Gorshin went back to bed and pulled the blankets up to his chin. He didn't want to turn off the light. He didn't expect to fall asleep but he did. Sometime during the night he woke up with the light glaring in his face and thought, what's that damn light doing on? Half asleep, he reached out and turned it off.

He dreamed; the locomotive was coming at him, full speed. It thumped and then started to howl. Peculiar sound for a locomotive to make, sounded more like a dog howling.

He woke up. He wasn't dreaming, a dog was howling and it was Charlie. Then a harsh rasping bark was cut off in midstream. He leapt out of bed and stumbled toward the door. It was very dark, there was no moon. But he knew his own house well enough to get around without light. At least he thought he did until he bumped into something which shouldn't have been there. A bright blaze of light blinded him and the stars came out in his head.

When he woke up he'd lost track of time and space. He was surprised to find himself on the landing at the top of the stairs. His head was killing him. Then he re-membered. Charlie! He got to his feet and almost dropped again. He felt around and found a lump and something sticky in his hair. He remembered hearing Charlie howl and then rushing through the dark. He must have tripped and hit his head and knocked himself out cold. As fast as he could, he ran down to the kitchen.

Charlie's blanket was in the corner where it always was. Only Charlie wasn't on it.

"Hey, Charlie?" he called, his voice sounding shaky. He turned on every light in the house and looked everywhere, even in the closets. Charlie was nowhere. As a last resort, he checked out the cellar although the door had a catch lock on it and was firmly shut. It was a nice cellar for a bomb shelter or keeping survival supplies. It had no windows, only stone walls. There was no way in or out of that cellar. He went down anyway, thinking of how it would feel to find Charlie's poor dog body lying in between the tarps and metal cannisters of water and toilet paper. It was a small place. The flashlight beamed around. Charlie wasn't there.

He went back upstairs and checked all the doors and windows again. Everything was still locked and bolted. Nothing looked disturbed. He went outside with the flashlight and looked at the ground under the windows. Nothing seemed trampled or stepped on.

He was badly shaken and that last yelp of Charlie's was still ringing in his ears. He supposed he wasn't thinking straight when he went to the phone and dialled Larry Pepperpot, the Police Chief. He only knew he was full of pain and grief and he was mad.

"Your dog?" Pepperpot, officially known as Doc Pepper to all and sundry, said. "Did you say your dog?" Gorshin reiterated and heard a stifled yawn. Doc liked good meaty things like murders, only there was never much in the way of murder in Sawtruck.

"Ayuh," Doc said sleepily. "You go to bed now,

George, we'll be by in the morning." Gorshin hated to be called George.

"Even an old dog has a few tricks left in him," Doc chuckled and hung up. Gorshin hadn't even had a chance to tell him about his head. He might have a concussion but Doc wasn't interested.

Gorshin sat by the phone until the sun rose. He felt very lonely. So lonely, in fact, that he thought of calling Clare. Good grief, he thought, if there was one thing in the world that Clare wasn't interested in, it was Charlie.

In the morning, as promised, Doc Pepper came rolling up the driveway in his brand-new police cruiser that looked as if it had just been washed and waxed.

"Now what's this about your dog?" he asked with a smile. But Gorshin was already thinking of something else.

Something much more frightening.

8

"A dog," Grepp said. "These kind of extras I don't need."

Farn was scratching the animal behind the ears. The dog looked unhappy and very tired.

"We'll get rid of it," Grepp said.

Farn stopped scratching. The dog looked relieved.

"He's a nice dog," Farn said.

"It makes no difference whether he's nice or not nice, we have to get rid of him." Grepp could see he was not making himself clear. "Kill him," he added so there could be no mistake.

Farn's mouth hung low, he looked as miserable as the dog. The two of them were standing there, woeful.

"I don't understand the point of a dog myself," Grepp said. "But, aside from that, we don't need such complications."

"He's not complicated."

"You don't understand me, Farn, dogs have big mouths, they bark, all that kind of thing. Makes a mess. I don't want a mess. Kill him."

Farn blanched at the words. Grepp changed his tone. "We'll do it quickly and painlessly. The dog won't know what's going on."

"He already knows," Farn said. The dog was shivering.

"He's a dog! Stop overestimating."

71

"He won't make any noise."

"Is that so?" Grepp asked, his voice cooly superior, far above such sloppy sentiment. "Have you asked him? Perhaps you could also ask him a few more questions while you're at it. Save us a lot of trouble. In fact, we could ask him to handle the whole operation, maybe?"

Farn tried to resume scratching the dog's ears. But the animal wasn't interested. It walked away and stood in the corner.

"You said nobody would get killed," Farn whined and he got down on his hands and knees and crawled toward the dog.

"A dog isn't somebody. He's a dog!" Grepp was beginning to feel impatient. "The whole reason the dog is here right now is because he made noise," Grepp reminded him. "The whole reason we are back where we started from is because of that dog's big mouth."

"We'll put him in the tunnel," Farn offered. "Nobody will hear him down there."

Grepp looked at the two of them in the corner. Farn was making a fool of himself.

"Get up," Grepp said. "Get up on your feet."

"The dog might help," Farn said, brushing off his skinny knees. "We could use him."

Grepp snorted.

"We could," Farn continued hopefully. "We could write one of those notes for ransom."

Grepp snorted louder. "You do that with people, not dogs."

It was Farn's turn to snort. "You have no understanding of the human race. People like dogs. They get attached to them. They feel close to dogs, there's no telling what they might do for the sake of a dog they liked." Such a long speech was unusual for Farn. But Grepp wasn't going to be moved by histrionics. Anyway, he liked to make all the decisions.

"Listen," he said. "Put the dog down in the tunnel for the time being. I don't have the stuff right now anyway."

"What stuff?" Farn wanted to know.

"The stuff, the stuff, the nice painless death. Put the dog away, I'm sick of him looking at me that way."

Farn smiled a little but not so much that Grepp would change his mind.

"I'll bring you something to eat," he told the dog when they were alone in the tunnel. "Don't worry about anything." He tied the dog with a thick rope and made sure the knots were secure.

"I'm sorry," he told the dog, "but it's necessary."

The dog was noncommittal. He stood, his head lowered, his tail drooping, his eyes watering, and watched the door close on Farn. His ears pricked up at the sound of a bolt sliding home. He sighed, sat down, rolled over on his side and shut his eyes. He fell asleep and had a bad dream, all about Gorshin and all the things Gorshin didn't know.

When he woke up sometime later, he began to chew the rope, slowly and very furtively.

9

Hunched over the small table, wailing sitar melodies assailing his ears, exotic brews sloshing in his stomach, Baker found himself fluctuating between meek hopefulness and blatant disbelief. Furthermore, he couldn't understand a thing the chick was saying. In order to salvage at least a portion of his sanity, he withdrew into a cocoon of private thoughts, pretending he was somewhere else. But the girl's voice kept breaking in, shattering his comfortable visions of Lear-Jets, casinos, hot dames with plunging necklines and laser guns that disintegrated tall buildings with a single swipe. The sweat that was trickling coldly down his body made him shiver.

Coincidence, he told himself, nothing more. A chick on the make (after all he was a reasonably good-looking guy) would use anything as an excuse to pick him up. It was probably one of her standard opening lines to tell a guy he was being followed. Mother-Supergirl to the rescue. It took him unawares, that's all. Nothing but a coincidence that she should have used those words, how could she have known that he was the exception, that someone or thing was always following him? Just a coincidence, forget it. He shifted in his seat, his ass was getting tired. He reached for his martini and thought about getting out and making the plane for Miami.

Mary watched him, thinking his eyes had suddenly gone funny again. The cappuccino was a mistake. They already had three cappuccinos and one was enough for anybody. Usually she drank espresso with a sliver of lemon. But the Pizza Kid had ordered cappuccino. He probably thought it was ice cream.

At first he wouldn't tell her his name. As soon as they sat down at the table Mary introduced herself, offering her hand. The kid looked embarrassed when he shook hands and he mumbled his name was Clint. Well, it was possible, but her instincts told her he was no Clint. So far it seemed like he didn't know nothing from anything. He was lagging behind the times somehow and he kept posing as some kind of big-shot gangster type, or at least he tried to. Every once in a while he would go off on some mental trip and start flexing his lip like Bogart.

"Hello," she said, waving her fingers in front of his eyes. He didn't even blink.

"Huh?" he said. Delayed reaction.

It was like pulling teeth, trying to make a few sounds become words. Frankly, she was getting tired. Nobody was *that* interesting. Staring off into space with a slightly pained expression around the eyes was a self-conscious act. Why was she bothering so much anyway? She could see he wasn't her type. Not that she had to have a special type, but she did like a little communication. Maybe because he had looked so fruity, she had hoped for too much. Something different, she thought, unlike the usual hip repartee she got from the swingers. The one-syllable yeah-man syndrome. A couple of ughs and aghs and the next thing was let's make it. And if she asked Why? which she felt was a basically simple question, they said Why not? Like she was supposed to turn on her libido like it was some kind of machine. She supposed it was Pete's fault, for bringing her up that way. He never made a big deal about sex with her, like she had all the facts when she was seven and they had just been getting refined over the years. Pete never told her not to go to bed, he never gave her any speeches on sin and virginity, although he spoke at length about V.D. Instead he told her, "Have a relationship. Get to know each other first so you know if you like each other. You know what I'm talking about, Mary?" He made no secret about Sondra. If he wasn't coming home he'd call and say, "I'm staying with Sondra." He would have preferred Sondra to come and stay with him, but she didn't like having to take a bath in the kitchen. Maybe it would have been better if Pete hadn't been so liberal. The result was that Mary was too particular. The girls she knew at school spent their time popping birth control pills and chalking up their experiences. It all seemed passé to Mary. She felt like a jade. One day a girl in her class came to school hysterical because her mother had found her pills. Pete would never get mad about birth control pills. In fact he often asked her if she was taking them. "Listen, Mary," he said, "you take care of that kind of thing yourself, you know what I mean? Don't trust these guys, I should know. They tell you they got a rubber in their wallet, don't you believe it. And anyway, it's probably full of holes."

So where did it get her? Where did it get anybody? They were all hung-up, spending all their time making plans for the next big thrill. She wanted to do something important and meaningful. And it wasn't going to bed with some guy she picked up. Now this kid, this so-called Clint, for instance, he didn't want to talk about anything. But he was different in one respect. He wasn't on the make either, and that was refreshing. She couldn't help feeling that if they could communicate, they might have a lot in common.

"Listen," the Kid said suddenly, "do you have a cigarette?"

"I don't smoke."

He looked at her like he never heard of such a thing. "You don't?"

"No."

The conversation fell flat. Anxious to keep it going, Mary asked, "Do you smoke a lot?" It wasn't a particularly scintillating question, but at least he might answer.

"Why?" he asked, bristling defensively.

"Well, well because, you know, smoking does all kinds of things to your body."

"Like what?"

"Well, your blood pressure and your heart, it can

change your pulse rate; and then our lungs are bad enough with this pollution we're breathing in every day without adding cigarettes to it, besides." Mary felt this wasn't exactly the kind of answer he wanted to hear, but, after all, he *had* asked.

"Oh," he said, "you're one of those."

"One of what?"

"One of those health-food freaks."

"Listen, I just don't smoke, okay? If you want a cigarette, you'll have to buy your own because I don't have any to offer you."

"You wouldn't want me smoking in front you, some of it might get in your lungs."

"I don't care what you do, you can smoke yourself to death in front of me if you want to."

"I have a friend who believes in all that stuff, organic food, homemade bread, the works. But he doesn't moralize on it all the time. If people don't want to agree with him, he doesn't put them down."

"I wasn't putting you down."

"But you did tell me smoking was bad for my health. I bet you eat all that granola and brown rice, don't you?"

The conversation was somehow going wrong, but Mary wasn't going to placate him just for the sake of talking.

"Yes I do, but I eat other things too, and anyway, I'm not telling you what to eat. I'm not even telling you not to smoke. I just told you to buy some cigarettes, didn't I?"

"I'm familiar with that kind of inverted reasoning."

Mary was momentarily speechless, trying to fathom this sudden paranoia.

"I bet you take a lot of vitamin E," he said, with gross overtones.

"I'll tell you what I don't take," she said.

"Yeah what?"

"A lot of crap."

There was a big silence. She felt a little sorry for him, realizing he was just trying hard to play the Casablanca scene. And speaking of inverted reasoning, maybe the poor kid didn't have enough money for a pack of cigarettes and was just covering up by making a big noise.

"Oh forget it," she said. "Listen, to show no hard feelings, I'll buy you a pack of cigarettes."

"I've got my own money," he said sourly.

"Well I'm glad to hear it."

"You don't have to do me any favors. Where's the check? I can pay for my own coffee."

"Fine."

"I'll pay for yours too, you don't have to worry."

"Who's worried?"

"I know the game," he said, puffing up like a pigeon.

"Look, let's get something straight. I invited you without a catch. I'm perfectly willing to pay for my coffee, for your coffee, for both, whatever you want to do. But let me tell you, you have a lot to learn. Somebody should teach you."

Two spots of red stuck out on his cheeks. Mary sat there, looking him straight in the eye. "Why the hell are you so hostile?" she asked him bluntly.

"What are you talking about?"

"Well, I'll be glad to tell you, if you want to listen," Mary said, feeling the atmosphere had changed and he was vaguely receptive. "But first of all, let's cut the crap, okay?"

He made a gesture as if to agree. His eyes, for once, were in the here and now and not off someplace else.

"I don't know what kind of friends you have, or what kind of relationships you have with them, but they must be full of hangups, the relationships I mean. All I was offering was a little friendliness, a little humanity, you know? Contact. Nobody makes contact anymore, we're all running around in our private refrigerators, too busy to open the door and turn on the light. I have my opinions, you have yours. I'm not trying to change you or tell you not to smoke, just like I don't expect you to start telling me how to behave either. But we can sit and rap. Talk, without the hostilities, without the garbage that most people are feeding each other every day. All this shit about who pays the check; who gives a shit who pays the check? It's really irrelevant, isn't it? I mean, the whole boy-girl scene where the little Miss Prissy-Pussy doesn't know a nickel from a dime isn't relevant anymore. And do you know why?"

"Yeah, Women's Lib. Right?"

"Oh Christ . . ." He had possibilities, he was just not used to talking straight. Maybe he wasn't used to anything being straight. She had the feeling he was living in another world.

"Listen, let's take a walk, okay?"

He looked doubtful. "Yeah, okay," he said after some deliberation.

The waitress brought the check. There was an eyeful pause before his hand reached for it. Should I save him or will it be too castrating? Mary asked herself. She didn't laugh. "We'll split it," she suggested. "But I did say I invited you."

He looked forlorn. Mary felt an unexpected and unlikely rush of motherliness. Before it could go further she whipped out a five bucks and slammed it down. She stood up. Her bulk loomed over him and he seemed to wince. "You can buy me a pizza" she said, hurrying him toward the door, "later."

They were outside and both of them breathed relief.

"Let's walk over to the river," she said. "We can go sit on the pier."

It took a long time for him to unbend. But maybe the fresh air loosened his mind. His quiet words blew away on the breeze, she could hardly hear all of them. It took only a little while for Mary to see how he was. Self-deprecating about everything, making everything into a joke like he didn't give a damn. He was obviously a very alienated person. The thing she noticed most was that he didn't seem to have any real opinions of his own about much of anything. He kept on agreeing with her. It was like talking to an echo chamber. All of his hostilities seemed to have gone below the surface. As if he felt it was too much of an effort to fight back. But she didn't have the heart to trip him up with conflict anymore. It was too bad for him, really. She didn't think he had many friends.

They stopped at the end of the pier. The wind was strong, whipping their hair around their faces. There was a tantalizing smell of the sea. All around, people were talking, laughing, reading, playing with dogs, throwing balls, screaming at their children not to fall in the river. But he was like a permanent inmate of the isolation ward. She couldn't stand it any longer.

"Hey, is your name really Clint?" she asked him. The wind blasted her ears.

He mouthed something that she lip read as "What?"

"Your name," she shouted, "is Clint really your name?"

Who is this? What am I doing? Baker thought, for a moment precariously balancing on the edge of his sanity. I don't have to tell her anything. I don't have to answer these questions. What is this, an interrogation? He felt like telling her to get lost, go to hell. He was tired of all her bright ideas about every subject in the world. She was out to save the world and she didn't really know a thing about what was going on. She was big on dropping the hostilities, but what did she know of real hostility? What did she know about Slynack hostility?

"Yeah," he replied. "It's a name I use."

"You use? You mean like an alias?"

"If you want to call it that."

"Okay, you don't have to tell me your real name."

"That's not true."

"No, honest, you don't."

"I mean it's not true that you don't care if I don't tell you. You really want to know, don't you?"

"No, I don't."

"Why did you ask then? Why did you bother to ask the question if you don't care."

"Forget it, okay?"

"No, I'll tell you my name if it means so much to you. It doesn't matter to me if you know my name or you don't know my name."

Mary pulled her hair out of her mouth, strand by strand. She turned her back on the wind and it all blew in again. "Well?"

"Well what?"

"Well what's your name if you're so anxious to tell me."

"What do you have, a thing about names?"

"I think they're interesting, that's all. You just didn't look like a Clint to me."

"I suppose you look like a Mary. The minute you walk in a door everybody says Mary, right?"

"How the hell do I know? It's my name and I'm used to it, I can't tell if I look like a Mary to myself or not. Anyway, Mary is one of those names people don't ask about, you know, it's just a name."

"And Clint, that's not a name?"

"Well it's different. Maybe if you were a little kid about five I'd think your mother named you after that actor, Clint what's-his-name, but he wasn't around when you were born. It's a sort of corny cowboy name, you know, it just doesn't seem your type."

"So what name do you think my type is?"

"Oh I don't know, forget it."

"No, tell me, you've got all these theories, what would you say my name is?"

She looked at him, feeling foolish. How did she get roped into these idiotic conversations?

"I don't know, I haven't really thought about it."

"You thought about it enough to decide it wasn't Clint."

"Okay, okay. George."

"George!"

"I'm sorry, I guess that's not your name, huh? You probably hate the name George."

"No, no. It's just strange you should pick that particular name."

"Yeah, well, I guess it's not as exciting as Clint."

"My name's Baker."

"Baker? Are you putting me on?"

"Baker Dilloway."

"So, with a name like that, why the hell bother to say your name is Clint?"

He opened his mouth. And closed it. Turned and stomped off.

"Hey . . ." He kept on stomping.

"Hey, wait a minute." Mary ran after him, trying to catch his arm. He shrugged her off. But she kept pace with him.

"You know what?" she asked, puffing a little, he was walking so fast.

He didn't answer.

"I want to apologize."

He turned and glared. "Don't bother."

"I want to apologize for asking you that. I mean, I should have accepted what you said. If you want your name to be Clint, it's your business. I shouldn't have questioned it. I'm really sorry. Wait a minute, are you mad I said your name was George?"

He was walking even faster and Mary had to struggle to keep up. Too many cappuccinos.

"A person can call himself whatever he likes. I shouldn't have intruded. Names are personal, it's just these dumb theories I have, I guess people aren't interested in them. Look, if you want me to call you Clint, I'll call you Clint. Okay? Clint?"

At the end of a pier was a fence with a one-person-size doorway in it. For a few seconds they were both trying to squeeze into the opening together. Then Baker stepped back and offered her the exit with a sweeping gesture.

She stepped through and stopped to catch her breath. "I really am very . . ." she started to say, but he brushed quickly past and took off across the street. "Wait . . . Baker . . . Clint!" she called weakly. Her voice floundered under the West Side Highway, drowned in the boom of traffic. Skirting cars, she ran after him.

"What's the matter?" she asked.

He stopped so short she bumped into his back.

"Do you want me to tell you?" His face was flushed, his hair ruffled. He looked less like a fruit all of a sudden. She had to admit, he almost looked handsome. More of a man.

"Yes."

"You talk too much, you're a regular massacre."

"A what?"

"Pick everything apart until there's nothing left."

"I . . ."

"And furthermore," he stood very straight and he sounded very definite, like he had all his opinions intact, "you're bothering me."

Then he smiled, possibly for the first time, sweetly sardonic.

He walked away. Left her standing there.

Mary stood speechless for a second. She was angry, mad, but bursting with enthusiasm. "I knew he had possibilities," she thought, "I knew it." She watched him disappearing up the street.

He was gone. But it didn't matter. She knew his name, she knew where he lived. "I'm going to follow you,

Baker Dilloway. I'm going to keep on your tail!"

He had possibilities, he might even make a friend. And anyway, she had to follow him. With such an advanced case of paranoia, he needed all the protection he could get.

"Fat Sister Is Watching You. You don't have to worry about a thing." Tomorrow she'd get there early and see where he went to school. But in the meantime, she better get her ass home and make the usual excuses to Pete.

Up ahead, out of sight, Baker was thinking about Red (better looking and more class than the kook with the pink sunglasses). He didn't consider himself in the least bit paranoid. And he had successfully rationalized his recent (but only momentary) terror away. Coincidence, nothing more.

It was too late to make a Search now, the day was shot, so he decided to go home and do the math homework he had been putting off all weekend. He felt good though, even if he hadn't made any progress on the Slynack stronghold. It had been a waste of time with that broad, Mary, but on the other hand, she had been desperate to pick him up (she had *pursued* him). He could afford to spare the time to give the girl a break. Seemed like he was always being pursued. If not by Slynacks, then by dames. Feeling cocky, he strolled along 10th Street oblivious to the fact that a dark shadow was darting in and out of doorways behind him.

10

"I guess you're right," Gorshin said to Doc Pepper as he poured him a second cup of coffee and passed the cream and sugar. Doc liked his coffee thick and sweet. Lots of everything was Doc's motto. Lots of sugar, lots of talk, lots of murder too, if only he could have it. He was plainly bored with the law-abiding citizenry of Sawtruck. Which meant he had plently of time to sit around and shoot the breeze on a Sunday morning.

Out in Gorshin's driveway, Doc's driver and right-hand man, John Bones, was listening with one ear to the police radio and the other ear glued to his transistor, which sang him the latest hit tunes and broke up the monotony. Neither Doc nor Bones was in a hurry to go anywhere. There were others down the line of the meager police force to do the more menial tasks of handing out traffic tickets.

Gorshin tried to appear as relaxed as Doc, but inside he was tied up in knots, wishing to be alone.

"Ayuh, he'll be back in time," Doc said, guzzling coffee.

"Sure, sure. Sorry to have troubled you in the middle of the night that way, sort of lost my head, I guess."

"You see things with more perspective in the daylight," Doc said. "Must be the weather. Gives everybody ideas, even dogs. Downright sinful, this weather, ought to be getting cold and nasty by now." Doc's eyes were bright as a bird's and they pecked into Gorshin's sleepy face. "Shame you forgot you left that window open," he added, casually.

Gorshin laughed apologetically, trying not to sound nervous. "Yes, I know. Getting forgetful in my old age. Look, I'm sorry, I just made a big fuss out of nothing. Must be working too hard or something."

"That book again, is it?" Doc asked. It was common knowledge that Gorshin was writing a book on organic farming. He had let this drop early on, when he arrived in Sawtruck. It helped explain a lot of things, and people didn't get curious. Most of the populace assumed Gorshin made a modest income writing articles on gardening, horticulture and the like.

"What you need, boy, is a vacation," Doc said. "Go someplace and let off a little steam for a change. Too quiet up here in the hills, get you stir-crazy if you don't watch out. Got to be born to it, I always say, can't take up the simple life in middle age." After ten years, Doc was still reminding him that he was a stranger to these parts. "Go to one of those resorts," Doc went on, "have a high time." He paused. "Got a steady girl, do you?"

"No," Gorshin said, too quickly. But damn it, Doc knew everything that went on in Sawtruck. He knew

Gorshin wasnt seeing anyone except casually, to go to a movie, to have a cup of coffee. He amended, "Not steady, that is."

"There you are," Doc said, and leaned over the table confidentially. "What you need is a little female companionship. No good being alone *all* the time."

"Yes, well, you're right." Gorshin felt like a broken tape, you're right, you're right, you're right.

"How's your friend in Boston?" Doc asked.

For a moment Gorshin looked blank. "Oh, fine," he replied and gained time by stuffing his pipe with tobacco, "she's fine." Whenever Gorshin made one of his infrequent trips to New York, he told people he was going to Boston. It had become a habit, covering his tracks. He did it even when it didn't make any difference one way or the other. Whenever he went to New York to visit Clare and Baker, he said he was going to Boston. Another fact to satisfy curious minds and keep them away from the truth.

"Been up here quite a few years now?" Doc asked. Of course he knew exactly how long Gorshin had lived in Sawtruck.

"That's right."

"Thinking of staying on permanently, I suppose." In Sawtruck ten years was a drop in the bucket; if he stayed fifty they might consider him permanent. "Not thinking of going back wherever it was you came from?"

"I might stay, yes," Gorshin said, edging away from

the subject. But Doc started talking about cooking all of a sudden. "Good coffee," he said, "you do a lot of cooking? I don't. My wife, she does all the cooking, tells me it's not a man's job. But when she goes over to Clayton to her family, I sneak in there. Whip up a big batch of my chili. Ever tasted my chili?"

"Yes, very good," Gorshin said. To Doc, chili was an exotic dish from another culture.

"You write anything about cooking? If you write about organic farming you should include a few recipes, down-to-earth stuff, no preservatives, that sort of thing."

"I hadn't thought of that," Gorshin said, attempting to sound interested.

"Rounds things off, makes for wider appeal," Doc went on, and began to advise on recipes and how to write them so people could understand the directions.

When Doc got on a subject, he wouldn't let go. The minutes dragged by as Doc expounded. His wife might not let him do much cooking, but he still had a lot of opinions. Gorshin found his mind wandering and, without realizing, he was staring at Charlie's empty blanket. He immediately averted his eyes.

"Dog'll come back," Doc said, noticing. "Ever been married?"

"No," Gorshin said automatically, and then regretted it. Suppose Doc checked up? But then, why should he? It wasn't as if he had reported his wife missing, it was only his dog! And anyway, why all these unrelated questions? What did Doc have on his mind? Or was he only passing the time?

Gorshin prayed for something to happen, for some disaster to hit Sawtruck and take Doc's mind off wives and dogs and back on being police chief again. He hoped Bones was paying attention to the police radio out in the car and not getting too involved in the hit parade.

Doc's cup was empty. Gorshin made no move to offer him more coffee. They sat together in silence for a while, Doc's opinions having run out. Fires, bank robberies, floods, catastrophes, Gorshin thought, anything to get Doc out of there so he wouldn't start noticing things, like, for instance, the way Gorshin's head was killing him from the bump he got in the night. Because Gorshin had already concluded that he had not tripped and hit his head by accident. He was pretty sure somebody had slugged him.

"Welp," Doc said at long last, pushing his empty cup a few inches across the table, "better be off."

Gorshin could hardly hide his enthusiasm. "Well, thanks again for all your trouble."

"No trouble," Doc assured him. "Now, you take my advice. Make yourself a reservation. Take a rest. Or better still, never mind the resting, go have yourself a good old-fashioned fling."

Gorshin accompanied him to the car. Doc took his time, aggravatingly sniffing the air, commenting on the marigolds that were still blooming so late in the year. He had some advice on weeds and a few pointers on organic farming himself. Then he stopped and looked over toward the house beyond the trees.

"How are the neighbors?" he asked.

"What? Oh, nice people, very quiet."

Doc gave him a long look. Gorshin felt a bead of perspiration make its way down behind his ear. He hoped Doc didn't see it.

"Now about the dog . . ." Doc began, shifting his bulk into a more comfortable stance.

"Hey, Doc!" Bones called suddenly, sticking his head out of the car window. "Ol' Man Biggin drove his tractor right into the side of the barn."

While one hand turned on the ignition, the other hand stashed the transistor radio carefully away under the dash.

"Ah well," Doc sighed. Old Man Biggin's poor eyesight was not exactly Doc's idea of excitement, but it was the answer to Gorshin's fervent prayers. He gave Gorshin a silent wave as he got into the car. He looked too serious, too thoughtful. Doc might appear to be a buffoon at times, but underneath he was shrewd.

Gorshin stood on the porch, waiting until the car drove off. It banked the curve and headed down toward the main road, skidding at the bottom. Bones had a certain flair for the melodramatic. Gorshin heard the siren start to wail.

Abruptly, he turned and went back into the house,

straight to his study. He began stacking all the papers and files, all the notes and typewritten pages of his book. He carried the stack out to the yard and put it into a wire trash burner he had inherited with the house. He preferred a compost pile to pollution, but now it was necessary to cause a little smoke. Very necessary. He struck a match and set the papers alight, fanning the flames and raking in air. The pages curled as the evidence was slowly reduced to ashes. He had been foolish to think he could safely put it all down in black and white. Someone had come for it last night and got Charlie instead. But they would be back. There was no safe hiding place now.

Trying not to cast too many nervous glances over his shoulder, he tended the fire carefully and when the whole mass was charred, he poured water on it and stirred until there was not the slightest possibility of recognizing what had been. Still not satisfied, he dragged the basket across the field and dumped it, spreading wet ashes on the ground, stamping them into the earth.

Before he went back into the house he stopped and looked at a patch of ground where one last thing had been hidden. He had buried it a long time ago and the grass had grown and covered all traces of his digging. He doubted anybody knew it was there, they had come into the house to search for what they wanted. He decided to leave the earth as it was. The last link, the last clue, was safe in its grave for the time being. And it was something he didn't yet want to destroy.

He shaved, showered and forced himself to eat. He dressed, putting on a turtleneck and a pair of slacks instead of his usual jeans. He pulled his suitcase out from the back of the storage closet and started to pack.

In a way, Doc had made things easier. Had, in fact, given him the go-ahead. By the time they realized he was never coming back to Sawtruck, it would be too late.

He put most of his clothes and odds and ends into his suitcase and filled a couple of cardboard boxes with books. He stuck the guitar into its threadbare canvas case. Stacking everything by the front door, he added his typewriter, the broken-down antique clock and the desk lamp. Then he made the rounds of the house, locking windows, checking lights, pausing in the kitchen to take a last look at Charlie's blanket before he stashed it in a cupboard. He turned off the refrigerator, emptied the ice trays and put the leftovers into a big garbage bag. He turned the water and gas off at the mains.

There was no time for sentimentality. A quick look around and goodbye. He'd make arrangements later on to sell the place and its contents. He had enjoyed himself here, it was a nice house. But it would never be quite the same without Charlie. He didn't believe in dog heaven but he hoped Charlie was peacefully dead and not suffering. No matter how hard he tried, his life always seemed to cause others pain. He had isolated himself from humanity for ten years, hoping to prevent just that, and now it was his dog. A poor helpless creature who wouldn't be able to tell them a damn thing even if he wanted to.

He put as much of the baggage as he could into the trunk of his car, leaving only the suitcase and guitar on the back seat where they would cause no suspicion. On the floor in the back he arranged an old lap robe, stuffing some pillows under it to give it shape. He hung his raincoat on the clothes catch. Its folds further obscured the mound on the floor, making it harder to see.

The only loose end was the telephone, but there was nothing he could do about that. It was Sunday, and shutting it off would be a giveaway too early in the game. He wouldn't have his phone disconnected for a short trip down to Boston.

As far as his bills were concerned, well, he'd have to get a post-office box somewhere and have them forwarded. It wasn't easy to disappear. Not if you wanted to be honest. There were phone, electricity, fuel bills. There was Mrs. Thwaite, and the bread that would be waiting for him tomorrow.

He shut the front door and locked it.

He drove down the driveway, stopping to unload the bag of garbage at the end where the garbage cans were stored in a wooden enclosure. Then he went straight on to Frank's Country Store. Frank always kept open on Sunday afternoons to catch the weekenders on their way back home. He was sitting in the shade of the garage doors, reading the Sunday comics. Doc was right, the weather was sinful, Indian summer was going on too long.

Frank saw the car and ambled toward him.

"Dog get himself home?" he asked. He would naturally know all about it. News travelled fast in Sawtruck.

"As a matter of fact," Gorshin said, "he came crawling back with his tail between his legs just after Doc left." He put his finger to his lips. "Don't want to wake him," he whispered; "gave him a couple of pills for the journey."

"Aye?"

"Taking Doc's advice," Gorshin said. "Would you mind filling her up, Frank? Im driving down to Boston, spend a week on the town. Have a fling, as Doc says."

While he waited for Frank to fill the tank, Gorshin found himself checking the rear-view mirror nervously. He felt like a criminal although he had done nothing wrong. It wasn't a crime to pack up and leave. Or maybe it was. Just up and leaving a bunch of people who had been friends for ten years, without offering them an explanation, without saying goodbye. That's always been my hangup, Gorshin thought, I'm no damn good at lying. And he wondered if Doc had believed the story about the open window, if he had swallowed it or had smelled a rat. He noticed Frank glancing in at the back seat of the car. Hopefully, it would look like Charlie was asleep under the blankets on the floor. And the suitcase was an obvious thing to bring down to Boston. He wondered if Frank believed him when he said he was going to Boston.

97

"Thought he didn't like to travel," Frank said, thumbing toward the back seat.

"He doesn't," Gorshin said. "That's why I gave him the pills."

"Take dogs in hotels, do they?" Frank asked. It was an innocent enough question. But Gorshin felt like he was being pumped.

"Staying with a friend," Gorshin said. "Anyway, can't leave poor Charlie on his own."

Frank looked thoughtful. He took Gorshin's check and listened to his explanation about needing extra money for the trip. He went back into the store to get the cash. When he came out his face was eager.

"Say, the wife and I, we'd be glad to look after the dog for you."

It was the last thing Gorshin expected to hear.

"Well thanks, Frank," he said, feeling like a heel. "But I wouldn't put you to the trouble."

"No trouble," Frank said. "He's a nice old fella. We'd be glad to oblige."

"It's very kind of you," Gorshin went on. "Really appreciate it. But maybe old Charlie needs a change of scene too."

Frank's face folded inward. He obviously thought Gorshin didn't trust him to take care of his hound. "No trouble at all," he insisted.

"I appreciate it," Gorshin said again. Frank was silent.

"Well, so long," Gorshin said. Frank nodded.

"I'll see you soon!" Gorshin gave him a big smile. He

waved as he put the car in gear and pulled away from the pump. Frank returned him a tip of the hand, his dour weather-beaten face in shadow.

Gorshin felt terrible. Damn, he thought, damn, why do people have to be so damn nice?

But as he quickly drove through the small town, he told himself he had no time or use for regrets. It was necessary and that was all there was to it. He'd had good times. Good people. He had not been on intimate terms with any of them, but he considered them friends.

He reached the highway and gained speed, heading for the interchange. It was like the repetition of an old nightmare. This was the second, no the third, time he had erased himself. Of course, there might be a better way. A way to end it all. Better, for instance, if he were dead, just like Charlie.

He drove toward Boston in the setting sun, wondering if it would make any difference, if things would change if one G. Gorshin ceased to exist. Probably not. Someone else would come up with what Gorshin had discovered. It would start all over again. And maybe this time temptation would win out. Because money and power were very tempting to some people. Gorshin wasn't giving himself any medals, but at least he hadn't copped out on the human race. Not altogether. At least he didn't think so.

No, a dead Gorshin wasn't going to save the world. The trouble was, a live one might just upset the balance.

The trouble is, Gorshin thought, I'm a gutless idealist.

11

The dames were crawling for it, they couldn't resist him. Baker allowed a swagger to ripple through his body (he had a good physique) and let himself into the hallway with his key. The front door was still locked; Lil was still being cautious.

He stopped and sniffed, as always, to make sure. The stairs seemed clear. No Slynack activity visible. He inched his way up, cautiously approaching the landings which were dark and lit with Lil's stingy two-watt bulbs. Everything was quiet. So he almost jumped out of his skin when the door on the third floor opened suddenly.

"Who's that?"

He jerked around, recognizing Lil's voice. "Me."

"Me?" She stepped out to get a better look. "You," she said. "I wanted to see you. Listen . . ." She beckoned him closer and whispered "I'd like to know what's going on." Her eyes rolled upward toward the fifth floor. "I caught that Katz up there. What's he doing up there, I'd like to know? Is the basement up there, will you tell me? Did it move upstairs overnight?"

"Uh?" Baker said. "Oh?"

"What's he doing upstairs, I asked him. Rude. He

doesn't give so much as a how-do-you-do. Me, I own the place, and he tells me it's none of my business. Have you ever heard anything like it?"

"Uh," Baker said.

"You better keep an eye on her. Hanging around your door."

"Who?"

"Who, who. That Katz. Outside your door. Listen, does your mother go out with him? I didn't think she was the type. Listen, I have nothing against it, I'm not prejudiced, but your mother is asking for trouble getting mixed up with Katz."

"I don't think she's going out with him," Baker said.

"Well, you see, what did I tell you! He has no business hanging around her door."

"Maybe he was coming to fix the doorknob or something," Baker said, feeling that Katz was entitled to some support. Privately, Baker didn't think of Katz as a particularly threatening character. Lil had a very low tolerance for any ethnic group except her own. To Lil, all Orientals were the dreaded tongs (she refused to eat Chinese food) and all people with skin other than her own bluish white were either musicians or dangerous characters. Since Katz was no musician, he naturally came under suspicion.

"What's the matter with the doorknob? Something's the matter? Nobody told me."

Baker started to inch his way up the stairs again.

101

"You're a big boy, you tell your mother not to get mixed up with someone like Katz. I'm not prejudiced, but I don't want any trouble here with these inter-relations, you know?"

"Yeah, I'll tell her," Baker said. "But I don't think you have to worry."

"If you have doorknob trouble, you tell me about it, you don't go to Katz."

Baker moved up a few more steps.

"You speak to Katz through me," she grumbled on. "I'm in charge of Katz."

She pulled her old gray sweater around her shoulders and banged the door shut.

It wasn't until he got to his own floor that Baker remembered the incident the night before. Could that have been Katz standing up there on the roof stairs? There was nothing really suspicious about Katz being up there, he often came upstairs to fix the toilets or the radiators, and it was Katz himself who had put the lock on the roof door. But they hadn't had any toilet trouble lately, and anyway, why would Katz run out on the roof without saying anything. Katz wasn't a big conversationalist, but he always said hello and made a few remarks about things in general if you met him. If it had been Katz up there last night, then he had to agree with Lil that Katz was acting in a suspicious manner. On the other hand, the man on the roof stairs had been all dressed up in an overcoat and hat and Baker hadn't been able to see his face at all.

Probably the two incidents were totally unrelated. Lil was always exaggerating. If he wasn't careful, he'd start thinking Katz was a Slynack in Katz clothing.

One thing he was certain of, he wasn't going to mention anything to his mother. She would get hysterical and call the locksmith to come install another lock and they already had two Segalocks plus a chain plus a bolt. The less his mother knew about people wandering around the hallways, Katz or otherwise, the better.

He let himself into the apartment and locked the door behind him (in deference to his mother). He'd have a little peace and quiet for a while before they got back from the park. Arnold would probably end up staying for dinner again, he couldn't afford to go out for a meal twice in the same day.

He went to his room and got out his logbook first so he could make the day's entries. Then he opened his math book and started fiddling around with the twelve problems he had to do by tomorrow morning. This led him into the inevitable mental diatribe against Simpson, who was not only the Headmaster of the school but the math teacher as well. Simpson was one of those people who was totally disconnected from the world. He had no idea what was going on outside his precious school. All the parents seemed to like Simpson, but Baker couldn't understand why. He was a stuffed shirt to the nth degree.

But thinking about Simpson got boring because it was always the same old things to think about. He allowed

103

himself a few moments to visualize Simpson's end at the hands of the Slynacks. Simpson would be standing in front of the class, intoning, as usual, in his monotonous baritone and he wouldn't notice the Slynacks at the window. The boys in the class would, however, and they would start to get nervous, pointing and whispering. This would make Simpson angry. (No talking in class, demerits for all of you!) The boys would tell him to look at the window and see for himself but he wouldn't just to be ornery. (Keep your eyes on your books!) Finally, the whole class would get up and run out because the Slynacks would be slishing and gurshing through the window frames. Simpson would get red in the face and his glasses would be askew and he would be banging his eraser and chalk all over the desk, screaming, Boys, come back here, come back, I tell you, double demerits for all of you! They would run out and lock the door and Simpson would suddenly notice the Slynacks slithering across the floor and he would call for help, pleading and begging and crying, and his glasses would be smashed and he would go down in a heap on the floor, covered by a writhing mass of Slynacks. (Help me please, boys, no demerits for the rest of the term.) Nobody would make a move until Simpson was devoured. Then they'd go on to the next class like nothing happened. Nobody would know what happened to Simpson. Not a trace would be left behind.

When he finished finishing Simpson off, he did one of

the problems and started on another one. But his mind kept wandering. What about this chick Mary, for instance? Too bad she was fat. She had a nice-looking face, no pimples or blackheads. He liked a dame with nice skin (Red never had a pimple in her life). But her hair was kind of dirty looking. She said her father owned a restaurant on MacDougal Street. It would be nice if his mother owned a restaurant, he could eat out every night and not have to wash dishes. His mother always wanted him to wash his dishes, that's why he liked pizzas.

Not that he really minded all the dish washing (mostly he ate peanut butter sandwiches on no plate), but he hated all the waiting around for hot water. They never seemed to have any hot water. Usually it went cold half-way through a shower. Or when his mother was washing her hair. She would have a whole head full of shampoo and the water would turn ice cold and she'd start cursing out Lil and the goddamn building and the crummy life she had to lead and when the hell was she going to get a break, for god's sake? If Baker made any helpful comments she got even madder, asking him what did he know about it, it wasn't him with a head full of shampoo and no money for a hairdresser. His mother's show was low budget and she didn't get a hairdresser thrown in. Her whole life was low budget, she said.

Once he heard Benny's mother say that "what that woman needs is a husband and father for that son of hers." She felt sorry for them because she thought they

105

had to live on peanut butter sandwiches (it was none of her business, he liked peanut butter).

Anyway, he figured his mother didn't have a husband because she didn't want one. That was okay by him. He didn't need a Frisby or an Arnold cramping up the place. Lots of guys at school had divorced parents, it was nothing new. But Benny's mother was behind the times, always talking about broken homes turning kids into junkies. That was bullshit. He for one thing was no junkie. He wasn't suffering because he had no father (was he?). Once he had a father, although he couldn't remember him because he died when Baker was only a baby.

He remembered only some tall guy looking down at him, a sort of Gorshin type with brown hair. His mother used to have all these pictures in an album only she lost it once when she was traveling on the road with this show, she said, but anyway what difference did it make, what was the big deal no having a father?

On the other hand, if his mother got married maybe she wouldn't be low budget anymore and he could get a bike. He couldn't really hold it against her if she wanted to get married, just as long as it wasn't a Frisby- or Arnold-type jerk.

Now Gorshin, it would be nice to have somebody like him around. He wished his mother would get Gorshin for a lover instead of Arnold. But Gorshin was some old friend of hers and purely platonic (he slept on the couch

106

when he visited overnight). Gorshin came down to New York only once in a while and sat around eating pizzas, which he couldn't find up in Sawtruck, Maine. But he was edgy being in the city, he didn't like the air or the people. He'd be hanging around in his socks, worrying about his dog, and then he'd be gone. Baker would wake up in the morning and look around and his mother would say, "He's gone, he left early." That would be it for another year or two.

Gorshin was real. He related to you like a human being instead of like Mr. Father-Figure who knows all, hears all, sees all, the way Arnold did. Arnold always looked at you like you had a few parts missing in your brain and needed all the help you could get. Gorshin was okay. He could live in anytime as far as Baker was concerned, but he guessed his mother didn't dig Gorshin that way. She didn't have anything bad to say about him, but she didn't say much good either. It was hard to tell if she was glad to see him or not. Maybe because he horned in on her social life and she had to cancel out Frisby or Arnold. But Gorshin seemed to like his mother a lot. He always brought her presents and asked if he could fix things or run down to the store to save her carrying the groceries. Sometimes she would make sarcastic comments when he offered to carry the groceries, like, "The delivery boy has been doing that for years, it only costs fifty cents extra." Other times they would talk and laugh the whole time he was there and she would be grouchy when he left. But

she never talked about him like he was a date or anything. In fact, she never wanted to talk about him much
at all.

Oh what the hell.

Sighing, Baker looked at the next math problem. Get
this done and maybe go to a flick to get away from Arnold.
Equations drifted in front of his bleary eyes. He felt his
mind wanting to go off on tangents, but he forced himself to concentrate.

He had to learn the stuff, completely, unequivocably,
impress it on his mind. He had very little time. They
would be coming for him. He had to imprint it on his
soul because the papers would have to be destroyed. He
alone would have the secrets, locked within his super-
intelligent brain, the only one on earth who KNEW. They
might use torture, hypnotism, to make him talk. He had
to be prepared for that. But that was okay, he had been
trained to stand up under torture. And if things got
rough, all he had to do was lift the false tooth at the
back of his mouth and let the capsule roll onto his
tongue. One bite, and it was all over.

Hopefully, of course, it wouldn't come to that. Because
Red would be waiting for him. It would break her up to
find out he was dead. His (handsome, sensitive) face
softened when he thought of Red. Then became hard
again, determined, almost brutal. He would be ready for
them when they came.

Methodically, steadily, he programmed his brain and

108

wrote the answers to the math homework down in the notebook.

Mary knew Pete would start in as soon as she walked in the door. And he did.

"So where the hell were you?" he asked, coming out of the kitchen with a dishtowel draped around his waist and a fork in his hand. She could smell the pungent aroma of spaghetti sauce from the pot on the stove. Pete always took a busman's holiday on Sundays. After spending all week cooking in the restaurant, he cooked at home. For a change. Experimenting all the time, currently with oregano and green peppers and tomatoes. His latest regret was that he wasn't Italian. Before, when he had the Hungarian restaurant, he lamented the fact that he wasn't from Hungary. And before that, he had a regular American hamburger joint and berated his parents for not coming over on the Mayflower. She wondered why he didn't just settle for what he was, a Greek, and open up a Greek restaurant for a little relaxing authenticity.

"So I was out for a change," she said.

"For a change she was out," Pete said, waving the fork around and following her into her room.

"If you want me to, I'll go down and clean up now," Mary offered.

"It's already cleaned up," Pete yelled. "What do you think I was doing all afternoon while you were out on the town?"

"Having a couple of drinks with Sondra, maybe," Mary said. She could feel the usual fight coming on. They were powerless to stop it. They just kept opening their mouths and putting their feet into them.

"Sondra washed the dishes!"

"I'm glad to hear it," Mary said. She took her sunglasses off and rubbed the bridge of her nose.

"She's glad to hear it," Pete said sarcastically to the wall.

Mary knew she should keep her mouth shut and just drop the subject. But instead she said, "It's good for Sondra to work with her hands once in a while. It makes for a more realistic relationship between you two, you know? It won't do her any harm to come down to your level occasionally."

"Come down to whose level? It's a comedown, I suppose, to help out; that's why you took off."

"I didn't say that. I didn't mean that at all. You always take everything I say the wrong way. You only listen the way you want to hear it. What I meant was . . ."

"Never mind what you meant . . . Miss Psychiatrist . . . has all the answers! Spare me, okay? Spare me all the analysis." Pete leaned back to sniff and see if the sauce was burning. "What you can do," he said, "is get hot with the books."

"I don't have any homework."

"Get hot anyway! Stay inside tonight."

"I'm not staying home for no reason. I have no homework, you can look at my books if you don't believe me."

"You can stay in because I say so. You take off without my knowing it, like this morning, I don't want none of that anymore. You hear that, Mary?"

"I'm not a baby for christ's sake."

"Yeah? Well, you're no psychiatrist either. You want to analyze me, get hot with the books. When you put up your shingle, then maybe I'll listen, not before. Until then you're still my kid, I got a responsibility. You've been goofing off lately. How're you going to graduate?"

Before Mary could tell him, he had raced to the kitchen to save the sauce.

Mary grabbed the door and gave it a slam.

She could always tell when Sondra had been working on him. Pete had a big thing about her graduating from high school and going to college, maybe because he never went himself, even as far as high school. But Sondra always added to it by giving him the conscientious-parent shakedown. She was probably pissed off about having to wash dishes with her gold chains hanging in the dish-water and her Ohrbach's fake furs getting all soggy. So she let off steam by taking it out on Mary. She did it under the guise of taking an interest. "I like taking an interest in your kid," she said to Pete, "I don't mind." Basically, Sondra wanted to get married, anybody could see that. Mary had to laugh. She knew all Sondra's hang-ups and Pete's as well. He wasn't going to marry her.

Pete would never do it because he had no intention

111

of changing. Sondra figured once she got Pete hooked she would make him over, make him get a nice apartment uptown, wear nice clothes, buy a car. She went with Pete because she thought he was an innovation, a diamond in the rough. And because he owned a restaurant, in her eyes he was some kind of big deal. But if she had to wash dishes, that was something else again.

Mary went over to the bed, kicked off her clogs and flopped down. She turned on the radio and spun the dial, attempting to tune in some decent music. All they played was crap these days. She was saving up for a really good stereo so she could listen to what she wanted, when she wanted. But somehow the money never seemed to get there. Pete wouldn't help, he always needed a new freezer or a new mixer or some gadget for the restaurant. Christmas was a gift certificate to Ohrbach's, an easy way out suggested by Sondra.

Sometimes she thought she would die if she couldn't hear some good music. Music healed, made her feel like believing in life when she had just about given up. Music cleaned out all the garbage in her head and put the fresh air back in. But the radio was hopeless tonight, just a lot of hog wailing pretending to be groovy when she wanted to hear Stravinsky, Ravel, even the Beatles.

Out in the kitchen, Pete dropped something and cursed. Pots clanged in the sink. The sauce was obviously not a success. The walls in the apartment were so damn thin, everything anybody did or said could be heard everywhere. You could even hear how long a pee someone was taking in the can.

She heard him washing the pots. Then silence. She had tuned in some semi-vile piano concerto and was beginning to relax when a clatter of hoofbeats and shouts of "Don't shoot," resounded from the living room. Pete had turned the TV on.

Mary felt like screaming. Instead she did some breathing exercises, willing herself into nothingness. Pete switched channels and the room rocked with the boom of canned laughter.

Christ, she thought. I'm lonely.

But that kind of thinking was verboten, never got you anywhere but down. So she closed her eyes and considered the aspects of leprosy as an allegorical disease while Pete guffawed louder than the TV set.

She needed to get some rest. Tomorrow she had to be up early and on 10th Street in order to catch the Kid before he left for school. No, not Kid. Call him by his rightful name. Baker Dilloway. Was that a name?

12

They used the tunnel to get to the house even though Grepp knew the man Gorshin had already gone. Still, it was better to be overcautious than sorry. The fat policeman might be hanging around, or somebody else unexpected. Unexpected things always happened when you least expected them. Below the surface of the ground there could be no surprises. They moved invisibly across the distance between Gorshin's farm and the old house that was their headquarters.

Invisibly but not exactly silently. The Thumper, a small battery-powered platform on wheels that could hold three men uncomfortably, might be swift but it made noise. Grepp called it the Thumper because of the sound it made on the rocky floor of the tunnel. Thump Thump Thump with some chuckas in between. Like a train.

Grepp was not in a good mood. There had been that nonsense about the dog again. When Farn wasn't looking, Grepp had planned to go down and cut the pest's throat. But Farn unfortunately caught him and started pleading. What about the painless death you promised, Farn had asked, eyeing the razor-sharp blade of the knife. Naturally, Grepp had no intentions of wasting time with

114

painless deaths, he had said it only to placate Farn. All death was painless in the final analysis anyway. Once dead, could you worry about feeling pain? A momentary twinge and it was all over. But Farn could not be dissuaded. In the interest of time, Grepp put the knife away. He wasn't giving in to Farn. But it was necessary for Farn to be in good spirits with his wits about him; functioning, not mourning over a dead dog.

It didn't take long to reach the other end of the tunnel and raise the trap door they had ingeniously constructed in the floor of the cellar. It was neatly hidden under some old tarpaulins, and a small amount of crawling on the hands and knees was necessary before they could actually stand up. As always, Grepp felt considerable pride as he emerged in Gorshin's cellar. "We build good tunnels, eh?" he said to Farn and slapped him on the back. Then he looked around and shook his head in dismay at the cellar's contents even though he had seen it all before. A waste to have so much stuff lying around unused and getting mouldy. But perhaps it was some religious foible of Gorshin's that required merchandise to be left in heaps all over the cellar. To Farn, the neglected wares and the dank atmosphere were like a tomb. He couldn't wait to get out and hurried up the stairs.

"A moment, Farn," Grepp cautioned. "Let us not be hasty." Placing a small sensor to his ear, he listened. "All clear," he said. There was no movement in the house above them.

The door leading into the house was locked, but it took

115

only seconds to open with their own key. They stepped into the kitchen. All the lights were off. In the corner, the refrigerator door hung open, revealing a barren and unlighted interior. It looked as if Gorshin had flown the coop. Grepp was not pleased.

They went directly to the study. Grepp's fears were confirmed. The desk was empty, the drawers bereft of files and papers.

"Search," Grepp ordered. "Search everywhere."

Using small flashlights, they searched. It took time, but there was no other way; they could not risk turning on lights to see better.

"He should have some curtains," Grepp complained as he stumbled in the hall. "All these bare windows are dangerous."

The search was fruitless. Pushing the last drawer back into the dresser in Gorshin's bedroom, Grepp said, "He knows."

Farn, having a tendency to be slow and rather sloppy in his searching, was still rummaging in the closet.

"Come out of there, Farn," Grepp commanded. "There is nothing here. We will have to resort to stronger measures."

Farn sat back on his haunches. Sometimes he didn't exactly follow what Grepp said, especially when they were out on a job. Grepp's voice changed and he didn't sound like himself anymore. He delivered speeches like an oracle and it was hard to understand.

116

"What?" he asked.

"Drastic steps," Grepp said impatiently. "It was naive to think we would have it so easy."

"Easy? What's been easy?" Farn asked, remembering the digging of the tunnel.

"We'll go back. I have to put in a call to Abraham."

"What for?" Farn asked. He was getting tired, his eyes hurt from trying to see with a tiny flashlight and he was worrying about the dog.

"A little ransom, Farn," Grepp said and his white teeth glittered in the dark.

"One of your ideas, wasn't it, Farn?"

"Yeah," Farn said. "I told you."

They went back to the cellar, but not before Grepp had satisfied himself that things looked as much as possible like they had before the search. They crawled under the tarp, pulled it carefully into place and locked the trap door. The Thumper chugged its way back through the tunnel, its one meager head lamp barely piercing the blackness.

At their approach, the dog started to howl.

"We must do something about that," Grepp said. "You'll have to face facts, Farn, the dog has to go."

"But," Farn said, not understanding, "what do you mean?"

"What do I mean, what do I mean," Grepp snarled, all patience gone. "I mean we shoot him in the head, knock him off."

"But we need him!"

Grepp, putting the brake on the Thumper and switching off the motor, gave Farn a long, concerned look.

"You feeling all right, Farn?"

"You said we needed him," Farn insisted.

"What are you talking about, what do we need a dog for?"

"For the ransom," Farn replied, very distressed. He had a feeling Grepp was losing his sanity.

As far as Grepp was concerned, Farn had lost his marbles long ago. He climbed up the ladder and pulled himself into the living room of the old house. He blinked in the sudden bright light. The windows of the room, and all the other windows of the house, were heavily draped. The lights were kept burning, even in the daytime.

"Sit down, take a load off your feet," Grepp said. Farn slumped into a chair, looking worried.

"Now look," Grepp said, speaking very slowly and clearly so Farn should understand, "we don't need the dog, understand? For nothing!"

"But the ransom," Farn said weakly. "I thought . . ."

"Kidnapping," Grepp said. "Not dognapping."

"But who?"

"You think Gorshin is going to turn over his brains for the sake of his dog? Maybe you're right, Farn, maybe people do go ape for dogs and whatever, but not so ape they're going to give us what we want just so they can have their furry friend back again. This is serious business, Farn, very serious."

Farn nodded meekly.

"In a case like this, a dog is expendable." Grepp took a deep breath and let it out slowly as he added, "Let's just hope a son is not."

Farn's face looked more confused than ever. "Sun?" he asked, "Son?"

"Gorshin's kid. We nab him and we're cooking with gas."

"But where is he? How do we know who he is? Are you sure he's got one? I mean, he's been living alone all this time, where'd he get a kid from?"

"The usual way," Grepp said. "He's got one all right. And Abraham's been keeping an eye on him."

Grepp chuckled. Farn's eyes were fairly popping out of his head. If there were any surprises, Grepp liked to do the surprising. He always had an ace up his sleeve. Grepp was the greatest. Just wait and see.

13

The day started like any other weekday. Baker switched off the alarm clock, disengaged his protective gear and got out of bed. He found his socks underneath on the floor and put them on. He shivered as he went to the john and came back to get dressed, giving the radiator a kick for spite. In the kitchen, his mother was pouring out orange juice with one hand and holding a script in the other. He said Hi and she said Mmmm. He kept quiet as he drank his juice, swallowed seven vitamin pills (his mother was no health-food freak, but she believed in vitamins, all kinds, A to Z) and ripped open a box of Rice Krispies. His mother liked him to be quiet when she was memorizing her lines. And she had no time to cook eggs on weekdays. She sat down across from him to have her coffee, but he couldn't see her face behind the script. Then she had a coughing fit and said, "Jesus, I have to stop smoking." About five minutes later she lit a cigarette.

He dabbled in his soggy Rice Krispies and watched the clock. Every morning, Monday to Friday, they had to have this race with each other. Baker tried to time himself so he could get out before his mother, but not so soon as to be early for school. His mother liked them to walk downstairs together so she knew all the locks were definitely locked and that Baker was definitely on his way to school. Otherwise, she said, she worried all day. She used to walk him right up to the school door but not anymore. He put his foot down on that one way back in the fifth grade, when he got sick of everybody laughing at him.

This morning was no different. He finished the cereal, took the bowl to the sink, made a lot of noise with the water and then tried to creep out of the kitchen before she knew what was going on.

"Wait a minute, I'll be ready in a minute," his mother said. Resigned, he went to get his books and check on the garlic putty around the window.

"Is the fire-escape window locked in there?" his mother asked him as she smeared on some lipstick at the hall mirror.

"Yeah, it's locked." As if he would leave it open.

"Baker, what's that smell? Don't you ever wash your hands?"

He wiped his fingers down the sides of his jeans.

"Did you brush your teeth and change your rubber bands?"

He mumbled. "You didn't. Go and brush your teeth. For god's sake, we spend enough on the orthodontist." He slunk off to the bathroom. "Besides that, you'll have bad breath," she called to him.

When he came out of the bathroom she was waiting at the door, keys in her hand, ready to secure the fortress.

121

They got to the ground floor and Baker was relieved not to see Lil mopping the hall. He didn't want her to start spouting off to his mother about Katz hanging around. She'd get nervous and want to meet him after school. Once, when there had been a robbery in the apartment below theirs, she insisted on having him take a cab up to the studio after school so he wouldn't be going home alone. But luckily, no Lil. His mother stopped to pick some gum off the sole of her shoe. As she was throwing a few curses around at Lil's stinking hallways, they heard a noise by the garbage cans. His mother, always on the alert for the rapists, froze and asked, "What's that?" Baker looked and saw a tall, dark sort of figure slipping behind the yard door.

"Only Katz," he said.

"Are you sure?" She peered down the hallway. "Why is he sneaking around like that?" Baker held his breath until they got outside in the street.

"Bye," he said.

His mother paused, looking back uncertainly. "That wasn't Katz. He always says hello, why would he run out the door like that?"

"Please, Mom, it's nothing, come on, you'll be late."

But her face was troubled. It was out of proportion, somehow. He wondered suddenly why she was always so upset, why she worried so much about him. The city was a cesspool, no doubt about it, but he had been going back and forth to school for years without mishap. It was only a few blocks away and it was broad daylight, the streets were filled with people, and besides that, he was no kid anymore. He was as tall as his mother and he had a decent set of muscles. He wasn't that helpless. Somehow the look in her eyes seemed strange. As if she were not just worried about the usual stuff, as if there were something bigger on her mind.

"Okay," she said, and seemed to shake herself back into shape again. "Bye, see you tonight."

They turned in opposite directions, Baker going toward school, his mother going up Hudson Street to get the bus uptown.

He was walking along casually but his alert was on. The Slynacks knew his route to school and, even though they probably wouldn't make a move in the street, he had to watch himself. He glanced into a shop window to check out the rear and he saw HER. He was so stunned, he stopped dead in his tracks and turned around.

"Oh, hi," she said, and he was pleased to see she looked a little embarrassed.

He waited, expecting some kind of explanation, but she came up to him and just stood there, smiling. "I guess we're going the same way," she said.

"I doubt it."

"Well, I see you're heading east and that's the way I'm going," she said, still smiling. She pushed her glasses back up her nose. "Mind if I walk along with you?"

"I thought you said you lived on MacDougal Street,"

he said. He started to walk, only because if he were late Simpson would give him a demerit and he already had enough demerits for six detentions.

"Oh," she said and he thought she sounded a little unsure of herself. "I do, but I stayed with a friend last night. Over there," she said and made vague motions toward some buildings across the street.

"Another coincidence," he said.

"What?"

"Nothing. I'm in a hurry, do you mind?"

"I like to walk fast myself," she said. "Keeps the fat cells busy," she added and slapped at her rear.

"Say, was that your mother I saw with you?"

"How did you see my mother if your friend lives over there?" he asked. She didn't fool him, he knew these broads, they made up any excuse just to tag along after you.

She laughed. "Not doing too well today, I guess. Oh well. Actually, I did stay with a friend, and I was passing when I happened to see you come out with that woman. Hey, she's not your mistress, is she? I mean, don't get me wrong, she's pretty nice to be somebody's mother."

Baker decided not to answer. He felt a little annoyed at her making allegations about his mother, but on the other hand if she wanted to think he had a mistress, well, so let her think it. He took a quick look around to see if anyone from school was nearby. He wouldn't want them to see him walking with this dame, he'd never hear the end of it.

"I hope I'm not intruding or anything, it's just that, well, we do know each other and why not share the morning?"

"I said I was in a hurry."

"Okay, okay, I'll get off at the next corner. I can take a hint."

They plodded on, Baker trying not to get too close.

"You know," she said, as they neared the corner, "I didn't want to bring this up, but I think there's something you should know."

"Oh yeah, what?" He hoped she wasn't going to start in telling him she was in love with him or something. He couldn't stand that.

"Well, I mean, I really hate to mention it, but if I don't then I'll be agonized if anything happens."

"So mention it, but hurry up, will you."

"Well, you know that guy I said was following you yesterday? Now don't get shook, it's probably nothing, but you know I said someone was following you in the subway? Well, I know you probably thought I was giving you a line or something, but he really did seem to be following you . . ."

"Come on," Baker said. He didn't really want to hear about it, he had solved that problem yesterday. She was right when she said she thought he thought it was a line. Just like this was probably another one. But something in him started to crawl around, making him feel funny.

"Okay, but don't look so nervous. The guy I saw yesterday in the subway was hanging around your front door this morning."

"Oh come on," Baker said and gave an impatient shrug.

"And not only that . . ."

"Listen. How come you saw this guy? Like how did you happen to be standing around watching some guy in front of my building? I thought you said you were just passing by when I came out. There was nobody there but me and my mother." Oh shit, he blew that one. But he was remembering the shadowy figure by the garbage cans.

"Never mind that for now, okay? Let me finish. This same person was in your building the night before also."

"The night before? I didn't even know you the night before! What night?"

"Saturday night," Mary said apologetically.

"You were in my building on Saturday night? I never even saw you before yesterday and that was Sunday. What's going on?"

He was sure of it now, she was some kook who had the hots for him so bad she would stop at nothing. She probably saw him around the neighborhood and asked who he was. He'd have to change his address, get an unlisted phone, have the boys take her for a ride and dump her in the river. Cement shoes, that would get rid of her once and for all.

"I have to get to school," he said quietly. He needed time to think. Because there was another possibility. She knew something. Could she be a Slynack? Was it happening? All the things he'd imagined, all the time he had been thinking the Slynacks weren't ready yet! He didn't like to believe it, but it had to be a possibility. Because if it wasn't possible, if this wasn't part of a Slynack Plan, then what had he been protecting himself from all these years? For a shocking, ice-cold moment, Baker was forced to look at the truth: were the Slynacks really real? Had he always half-hoped they were a figment of his imagination? His blood curdled. He started to tremble.

"Oh God," Mary said. "Look, it's probably nothing. He probably lives in your building, right? He probably wanted to tell you something in the subway and I misinterpreted. I'm sorry. I guess I made a big thing out of nothing, huh?"

But Baker wasn't even listening to her. He was thinking of the man in the overcoat on the roof stairs, of Lil telling him that Katz was hanging around the door.

Mary started to walk away. She looked very upset.

"Hey wait," he said. "Come here. This guy you saw, what was he? I mean, was he black or white?"

Mary turned back, surprised at his vehemence. "What does that have to do with it?"

She put her hand on his arm. "Look, I told you I was sorry. Don't even give it a second thought anymore, okay? It's just me, me, I'm the one who took it all the wrong way. I don't want to get some poor innocent man in trouble because of me. Forget it."

"Just tell me, black or white?"

"I don't like making value judgments on the color of someone's skin. I mean, you wouldn't ask me . . ."

"People do come in different colors, just like hair; you wouldn't get so damn uptight if I asked you what color hair he had. You're about as good as Lil."

"Who's Lil?"

"Cut the crap," Baker said so loud that a few people stopped and stared at them. "What color?" he asked, more quietly.

"Well, he was in this overcoat, the first time that is, and again this morning, I could hardly see him. But I'm sure it's the same one because of the hat, he had this strange hat on, I mean, nobody wears hats like that. I wasn't sure the first time, but then I started thinking about it and I figured no two men could have the same stupid hat. He was sort of deep brown."

Katz? It seemed ridiculous for Katz to have been running after him in the subway, but then on the other hand, he had seen Katz in the subway before. Part of it could easily be explained. Katz did work in the building, so it was natural that Mary should have seen him there. Katz did know him, so he could have wanted to tell him something in the subway, although Baker couldn't think what. None of that was strange, not really. The part that couldn't be explained was why Katz should start hanging around their apartment door. And why he didn't say anything the night he was on the roof stairs. If it had been Katz up there, wouldn't it have been normal for him to have said something, anything,

128

when he saw Baker looking up? Instead he had run out on the roof. That was suspicious. *If* it was Katz. But Lil had told him it was Katz. So it must be Katz.

But Katz never wore a funny hat. And Baker couldn't remember seeing him in an overcoat. Still, everybody had an overcoat. Why shouldn't Katz have one?

"I better go," Baker said, torn between further questioning of Mary and Simpson's demerits.

"I hope you'll forget all this shit," Mary said. "I hope you won't hold it against me."

Baker backed up as she extended her hand. He still wasn't so sure about her. He wasn't sure of anything anymore. Lousy Slynacks, he thought, why did I ever get mixed up with them?

"I sure would like to know what's really going on," he said, giving her a piercing stare to see if she gave herself away.

Mary stared back blankly. She watched him cross the street and run. She followed. Not because she was following him, but because she was near enough to the East-Side IRT and wanted to take it. She couldn't help it if she just happened to be walking on the same street, could she? But she hoped he wouldn't turn around and see her. He was a paranoid all right, she should have known better than to tell him anything. She didn't even know why she did. It was a stupid mistake and she probably queered any sort of relationship between them. Her tough luck. As usual.

Feeling bad, she decided to go on sabbatical and give

up the tail game for a while. As penance, she'd go to school every day this week and never look at another face. She remembered Pete's words, "Who do you think you are, a psychiatrist?" She felt sorry for Baker and for getting him so upset, but Pete was right, what could she do about it? Except maybe mind her own business.

It was only by chance she saw what happened. She had no intention of sticking her nose into Baker Dilloway's business again, but it happened right in front of her eyes, she could hardly have just ignored the whole thing.

She had been keeping her distance behind him and he had been heading toward two big brownstones which she assumed were his school, even though they looked just like the rest of the houses on the block. But the doors were open and a lot of boys, all sizes, were going in. She slowed down so he could get inside before she passed so he wouldn't think she was following him again.

But instead of going up the steps, Baker paused and turned around and went over to a car that was parked at the curb. Mary couldn't hear but she guessed that someone inside the car had called him over. He didn't look upset or anything, but all of a sudden his body seemed to shake back and forth in a funny way and before Mary could blink an eye, he had disappeared inside the car. The door slammed and the car took off fast, jumping the light at the intersection. It all happened so quickly that nobody else blinked an eye. The schlumpy kids

130

kept right on going into school and not one of them turned around.

"Hey . . . hey . . ." Mary yelled, but nobody paid any attention to her.

"Did you see that?" she asked a woman who was passing by. "Did you see what happened?"

The woman gave her a dirty look and crossed the street. A couple of other people gave her a wide berth and she realized she was sort of running around in a circle, waving her arms. She stopped.

"I sure would like to know what's going on myself," she said to nobody.

Then she did a weird thing. She continued walking to the subway. As if nothing had happened. Maybe because she couldn't really believe anything had happened. It was too unreal. If she didn't watch out, she was going to make another one of her misinterpretations. If she didn't watch out, she was going to be sticking her nose in again.

Her mind must have short-circuited and she found herself waiting for the train in a state of mental limbo. She felt sort of numb. When the train came she pushed her way in. There was no seat and she was squashed against the door. Snap out of it and start thinking, she told herself. But she couldn't think with all these bodies leaning on her. After 42nd Street the crowd thinned out and she could breathe. She beat a man to a seat and as soon as she sat down her mind started churning. It took time to get the mishmash sorted out so that she could look at the whole incident sensibly. By the time she had drawn a few tentative conclusions, she was long past her stop. Oh hell, she thought as the train ploughed on into the Bronx, school can wait another day. This might be too important. This might be real!

And she wondered what the Kid had been so scared of.

14

"Abraham did it," Grepp said. "Success!" His face was beaming. He tore off the radio headset and rubbed his hands together excitedly. "Now we sit tight for a while. When we have the kid under lock and key, we send a friendly message to Gorshin."

"That's good," Farn said, trying to stir the sticky mass of oatmeal in the bowl he was holding. His cooking was not so good. He hoped the dog wouldn't mind. "Only, how?"

Grepp was pacing the room, his mind full of ideas on the best way to approach Gorshin with the news. He liked a creative challenge, it got his blood running.

"What do you mean, how?" he asked distractedly.

"How do we tell Gorshin?"

Grepp stopped pacing and turned on Farn. "We send a letter in an envelope with a stamp. Or a telegram. Or we make a phone call. Let me worry about these things, Farn." He noticed the bowl in Farn's hands. "What is that mess you have there?"

"Oatmeal."

"You've had your breakfast already, Farn. Where are you going with the oatmeal?"

133

"He's hungry," Farn said. He surmised that Grepp's mind was not really on the dog at this moment. "It will keep him quiet for the time being," he added, hoping to convey the idea to Grepp that it was only temporary. "Gorshin is gone," he said to take Grepp's mind off the subject more completely. "How do we contact him?"

"Not everyone is a fool, Farn," Grepp said sneeringly. "What do you think Klinc has been doing all this time?"

"Oh yes, I did forget Klinc," Farn said, easing himself across the room.

"All right, Farn, give him the oatmeal and get right back up here, we have work to do."

"Yes, Grepp. Certainly, Grepp." Farn hurried down to the tunnel and pushed the dish of oatmeal under the dog's nose. He was quick about it, not wanting to annoy Grepp any more than necessary. He was sorry he couldn't stay and comfort the animal with a pat on the head. But all he could offer was a friendly smile before he hurried away again.

In his haste, he failed to notice the rope. It had been chewed almost through, and the dog was cleverly sitting on his handiwork, as if he knew he had to hide it.

15

John Bones pulled the nondescript green Chevrolet up beside the phone box, bailed out and put in a call to the Chief. Luck seemed to be with him; the phone box was empty, but he didn't know how much time he had. He drummed his fingers impatiently as he waited for the connection.

"All right, Bones," Doc's voice crackled through. "How's it going?"

"He stopped for food," Bones answered. "Still heading generally southwest."

"Keep with him."

"I'll try, Chief, but it might get hairy. He's got company."

"Clarify, Bones, don't keep us guessing."

"Somebody else is on his tail besides me."

"Okay, we'll try to get a make on him."

Bones relayed the color, model and license plate number of the car he had observed tailing Gorshin. He could see the car now, parked in front of the diner. The driver had gone inside. He couldn't be sure, but he had a strong hunch that this was no planned rendezvous, that Gorshin was unaware he was being followed.

"Do your best," Doc said. "He's got to get to somewhere, he's not going to stay on the road forever."

"I hope not," Bones said, easing his sore back. Last night, while Gorshin had slept comfortably in a motel, Bones had spent the night in the car, unable to get much rest aside from a few catnaps. He had polished off his thermos of coffee and the sandwiches. He was hungry and tired.

"I wish I could get you some assistance," Doc said. "But you know that territory is out of my jurisdiction. I'm taking a hell of a risk sending you out on this as it is. But believe me, Bones, I lay my pension on the line this is no wild goose chase. We're going to come up with something and when we do, we hand it over."

Bones craned his neck out of the phone booth. Gorshin's car was still parked and empty. "I'm going to have to hang up pretty soon," he told Doc. "I may have to cut you off. But in the meantime, did you find anything at the farm?"

"Welp, I spoke to Frank for a few minutes, just casually. He tells me George was taking some advice I'd given him, gone down to Boston for a vacation, just like we originally thought ourselves. Took the dog with him, he says. I went up to the farm and had a look around. A little risky, breaking in like that, but then George and I are old friends and I was just making sure everything was shipshape while he was gone. He's cleared out all right, Bones. Didn't take everything but enough. All his

136

clothes, papers and personal possessions are gone. But I doubt he's going on vacation. And another thing, I'd be mighty surprised if he had his dog with him. Mighty surprised."

"Frank see the dog?"

"Not exactly from what I gather. You know how it is, Bones. By now he probably believes he did see the dog. I didn't want to get too picky about it. Time enough for that."

"And the Smiths?"

"Stopped in on them. Same old codger that was there the last time, he doesn't know anything. But I'm reserving judgment."

"Listen, Doc, I better go."

"Okay, Bones. Keep in touch. And, John . . ."

"Yes?"

"Take care of yourself."

Bones hung up and got back in his car none too soon. Gorshin came out carrying a paper sack. Food, no doubt. Bones could feel his mouth watering at the thought of it.

Gorshin pulled out onto the highway and Bones followed, allowing another car between them so that Gorshin wouldn't see the green Chevy right off. Before long the other car was following again as well. They made a nice procession. A dangerous one. Sooner or later somebody was going to start noticing somebody else. When that happened, all hell would break loose. Doc was a hard person to say no to. But Bones had his doubts

137

about the mission Doc had sent him on. Not that he doubted Doc. If Doc smelled a rat, there was usually a rat. He didn't doubt for one minute that Doc was on to something big. The problem was it might be too big.

16

It was starting to turn cold. It happened like that sometimes. A long autumn that was more summer than fall,
and all of a sudden, bang, you could smell the snow in
the air. Progressively, all afternoon, the temperature had
been dropping. The winter was coming on, and by five
thirty it was dark. Outside in the street, the streetlights
were burning with a steady pink-orange glow. Down in
the basement, it was darker than a rathole.

Maybe it had something to do with the change in the
weather. Katz was feeling low. Maybe it had something
to do with this lousy job he was on. He was lying low too,
down on the floor next to the boiler, trying to put some
life into the ancient machine so the people upstairs could
get a little heat. If Lil would keep out of the basement
and stop fiddling with the thermostat every five minutes,
he wouldn't have all this trouble. He had a B.S. and a
master's degree and for the past two years he had spent
most of his time fixing boilers, toilets, and trying to shore
up the dump and keep it from falling down. It was a
damn good thing his father had been a plumber.

He had only himself to thank. Oh sure, I'll take that
assignment, couldn't wait to get his ass up to New York

so he could be near Gwen. Lot of good it did him with Gwen. She thought he had no ambition. She was embarrassed to introduce him to her friends. Archibald Q. Katz, janitor. He couldn't tell her why. He told her he was writing a book and wanted to get the inside dope on the janitorial scene. But after two years she didn't believe him anymore. "Where's that book you've been writing, Archie?" And her pretty little eagle eyes gave his empty desk the onceover once too often. "I'd like to read that book sometime, Archie." He didn't blame her for losing faith in him.

"At least you could call yourself a super," she'd said the last time. "Or how about a maintenance engineer? That sounds pretty classy, doesn't it?" He wanted to tell her, right then and there. What difference would it make? The way things looked, he could be on the job for another ten years and nothing would happen. He was putting in for a transfer. He had to do something drastic soon. "I love you Archie," she told him, "but I'm damned if I'm going to be the janitor's wife. Taking out the garbage is just not my style."

He spent so much time around the garbage, he began to smell like a garbage can. And he'd thought he was going to make like James Bond.

He threw the wrench down and straightened up. Time to check on Dilloway. He should be home by now. Never could tell with that kid, though, he never came in the same way twice. Spent a lot of time running up and down the fire escape instead of using the stairs. Crazy kid had garlic all over his bedroom window. Maybe he was afraid of vampires. Anyway, nothing he did surprised Katz anymore. He was used to it by now. That kid didn't need protection, he needed a psychiatrist.

He wiped his hands off on a rag and stuck it into the back pocket of his overalls. Then, looking the epitome of the typical janitor, he climbed the stairs, a little scruffy, a little shiftless, none too interested in what was happening around him.

He could hear a commotion when he got above ground. Sounded like Lil and Mrs. Silvestri and the kid's mother, Mrs. Dilloway. They were upstairs somewhere, probably on Lil's floor. He lurked around, wiping doorknobs and spit-shining the mailboxes, keeping an ear out, expecting the argument to be about the heat and hot water. There had been no hot water all afternoon.

But he began to get a sense of the words. It was no argument about hot water. It had something to do with the kid, Baker.

"Well, I might be overreacting," Mrs. Dilloway was saying. "I just thought I'd ask if you'd seen him."

"Don't worry," Mrs. Silvestri said. "He's a big boy and boys can take care of themselves. He'll come home, six o'clock, seven o'clock. At midnight you start worrying, but don't worry now."

"I'm not really worried," Mrs. Dilloway said, sounding worried.

141

"Always in a rush," Lil said. "Always in or out. He needs a leash, that way you know he's on the end of it."

"Shut up," Mrs. Silvestri said. "Why make the poor lady upset?"

"So don't ask me. You asked me and I'm telling you."

"Whatsa matter?" a new voice broke in. It was Trotta.

"Nothing," Mrs. Silvestri yelled down the stairwell. "Mind your own business."

"I'm trying," Trotta yelled back. "But who can mind his business with this racket?"

"Look, I'm sorry I bothered you." Mrs. Dilloway's words were lost in the shouting match between Trotta and Mrs. Silvestri.

"Calla cops," Trotta suggested. "Whatsa bunch of you gonna do?"

"Oh no," Mrs. Dilloway said. "I think I'll go back upstairs now, in case he's trying to call me. Thank you."

Katz waited until the din subsided. He heard doors slamming and the general muttering ceased. Then he made his way up to the fifth floor.

It was a risk but he had to take it. He knew one thing, Mrs. Dilloway had sounded very concerned. It meant that she knew something more than she had divulged to Lil and Mrs. Silvestri. She had a reason to be upset, a better one than the kid's being a little late after school.

He tiptoed past Lil's door to avoid an unnecessary confrontation which would get neither of them anywhere. He paused in front of the Dilloway apartment, taking

142

a deep breath. He wouldn't blame her if she laughed in his face. How was it going to look when Katz, the friendly and not too efficient janitor, suddenly presented himself as the FBI?

He knocked, knowing the door buzzers were rarely in working order. There was an excited flurry of footsteps and then the door opened cautiously, the chain still engaged. He decided to play it cool at first. See what he could find out.

"Mrs. Dilloway? It's Katz."

"Ohhhh," she sighed, out of disappointment or fear, probably both.

"I heard you were looking for your son."

"Yes?" The voice was trembling.

"I wondered if I could help in any way."

"Did you see him this afternoon at all?"

"I'm sorry to say I didn't. He usually gets home from school before this, doesn't he?"

"That's the trouble," she started to say, then her voice cracked and she seemed near to tears.

"Trouble?" Katz murmured encouragingly. The chain was still on, they were talking through the small opening between the door and jamb. He wanted to convey his sympathy and concern, but he was afraid he might appear menacing, with his face peering in at her.

"He wasn't in school!" She almost gave way, but she realized she would be crying in front of Katz, the janitor! She sobered up.

"Are you sure?" he asked.

"I called his friends, well, these two boys he mentioned yesterday. I thought he might be with them." She paused. Evidently she was wondering why she should be telling all this to the janitor.

"And they said he wasn't in school today?" Katz asked. She shook her head.

"Mrs. Dilloway," Katz said, no longer in the manner of a janitor, "I think I know what's troubling you."

"What do you mean?" she asked, fearful again, a little affronted.

"I'm on your side, Mrs. Dilloway." He pushed the I.D. through the opening. "I think it would be a good idea if you let me in. In a moment Lil is going to be up here wanting to know what I'm doing."

She read the I.D. card, moving her lips. "Is this . . . I mean . . . I just don't . . ."

"It's real," Katz said. "You can call that number if you want to verify."

"Well I just don't . . . yes, come in, please."

She unlatched the chain and opened the door. He could tell she was still very wary of him. But the desire to find out something, to get any kind of help, was too overwhelming. She was willing to risk it.

"Are you really what this says?" she asked, understandably confused.

"I am." He shut the door behind him and waited. She handed the I.D. back and led him down the hall to the living room.

"Do you know . . . anything at all? I mean, were you here because of this?"

"I was assigned here, yes. They wanted someone around, just to keep tabs on the situation should anything arise."

"And it has, hasn't it? Just what I've been dreading all these years. Oh, I've been living with this for so long. . . . Baker never understood. I never told him. Maybe that was a mistake."

"Not necessarily. There was a good chance nothing would happen. And we don't really know if anything has."

"But if he wasn't in school . . ."

"It might not be so bad . . . he might have decided to cut classes."

She collapsed into a chair and took out a cigarette, fumbling with a match.

He held out his lighter.

"Katz!" she said, half laughing, half crying. "And I always thought you were the janitor."

"I was the janitor," he said. "And as far as anyone else in this dump is concerned, I still am!"

She buried her face in her hands. She looked worn-out.

"Suppose I make us a pot of coffee," he said. She nodded.

When he came back with two mugs of instant coffee, she had better control. "I wish I could agree with what you said," she told him. "But I have a horrible feeling it isn't going to be a matter of playing hooky."

"Well, I think we better have a long talk before we decide the best course of action."

She took the mug from him. "I haven't talked about this in so long. I don't know where to start."

"Why not try the beginning," he said. And he sat down and prepared to listen, stretching his legs and hoping he was going to have a chance to take off these damn overalls once and for all.

17

Abraham had done his job well and he was slightly irked by Grepp's attitude. Grepp was overconscientious, he wanted all the angles covered not once but twice, even three times. Go back, Grepp said, and hang around 10th Street and see if the kid's father shows up there. What for? That was Klinc's job. If Klinc couldn't handle it, he shouldn't be doing the job in the first place. Abraham was sick of the Village, and he had been looking forward to going up to Maine. Grepp had led him to believe that once the kid was nabbed, he could close down operations in this stinking city and get the hell out into open air. But no, Grepp needed him here, hanging around, probably arousing suspicion. When he voiced this concern to Grepp, Grepp wasn't interested. "Look like a bum," Grepp told him. "The Village is full of bums, one more won't be noticeable." So he bought himself a pint of whiskey and put it in his pocket, still in the paper bag. That's as far as his imagination took him, he couldn't think of any other props to make himself more bumlike. It would serve Grepp right if he got picked up for vagrancy, that would teach him to be satisfied.

He also got most of the shoe polish off his face which

147

was a relief. It was giving him a rash, that shoe polish. And it had been some job to get it off, he even tried bleach. But most of it was gone now. Grepp hadn't told him to discard this part of the disguise, he did it on his own initiative. If he was going to be hanging around the kid's building again, it seemed sensible to look different. Grepp didn't know all the answers, he only thought he did.

Feeling highly disgruntled, Abraham dragged his feet across Seventh Avenue, performing his bum act. He was nursing his hostilities, making the most of them. It helped to take his mind off the other thing. He felt guilty, when he let himself think about it, about the fat girl. He'd had all good intentions of telling Grepp about the girl, but when the time came he found he didn't want to. It would just be a complication, and he foresaw a longer and longer stint on the streets of Greenwich Village looming in front of him. He wanted to get out, go up to Maine, get his pay and take off. He had been planning to go to Canada. Well, fat lot of good it had done him. Now he had double troubles because if the fat girl botched things up, Grepp was going to have his neck for not telling him.

Of course, he wasn't positive. That helped. He couldn't be positively sure that it was her. It had looked like her. But he didn't have time to doublecheck. So maybe it wasn't her. Anyway, Abraham rationlized desperately, even if she did see the kid being nabbed, what could she do about it? Pretty soon everybody was going to know the kid had been taken. What could happen?

Abraham didn't like to think about what could happen. He just wanted his money and out. He never should have got mixed up with them in the first place. They were bad business, something weird about them, he couldn't put his finger on it but he sensed something. He was sorry about the whole thing. The kid was pathetic, scrawny and miserable. He didn't like sticking that needle in his arm. He hoped Boris would have it in his heart to show a little kindness on the way to Maine. But if he knew Boris, the kid wouldn't even get to take a leak.

Shaking his head with woe, Abraham leaned on a parked car and took the paper bag out of his pocket. He unscrewed the cap and smelled the whiskey. He didn't like whiskey, and he wasn't sure if drinking on the street was legal. He put the cap back on and put the bottle away again.

He had been hoping to go straight. No more jobs, no more hitting the gas stations for a few measly bucks. That's why Grepp's offer had been so tempting. A lot of cash for an easy job, one that wasn't even illegal. Just a little surveillance, Grepp had said. He didn't mention kidnapping. Just keep an eye on this kid, Baker Dilloway, follow him around and report. Nothing more. If Abraham had known there was going to be kidnapping he never would have done it. Kidnapping was a big offense, the Feds would get in on it. No, he didn't want to think what

149

would happen; going across state lines, he'd heard that was the worst thing you could do in a case of kidnapping. Grepp should have told him. It wasn't fair.

His new life in Canada seemed to be fading before his very eyes. He saw the years dwindling as he lived out his time in the pen. Life was too short. What did he want with kidnapping? He slumped against the car, all his hopes shattered.

Some young people walked by and one of them stopped and came back and put out his hand. Abraham took a few moments to realize the man was offering him a quarter. "No, no thanks," he said, feeling embarrassed.

"Take it man." The man's friends were laughing. "Hey, big spender," they called to him, "can you afford it?"

"Thanks a lot," Abraham said, to spare himself further hassling. They walked away, laughing and pushing at each other. He looked at the quarter in his palm. This might be what he would come to, begging in the streets. If he didn't dislike the taste of it so much, he'd be tempted to drink the whole bottle of whiskey.

He pulled his hat down over his eyes and hunched inside his overcoat. It was getting cold, it was not going to be any picnic hanging around for Grepp. For want of something better to do, he stared toward the kid's apartment building. He wasn't even sure he would recognize the kid's father if he saw him. Grepp had sent a bad photo and a wordy description written on the back of it. *Study this and destroy,* he had written. Like he was playing spies.

Lost in his depression, he didn't notice her coming. He was so shocked by the voice in his ear, he jumped.

"Hi there," she said. "How are you?"

He opened his mouth but nothing came out.

"Pretty cold for standing around out here, isn't it. Maybe we should go inside."

"Go on, get lost," Abraham said, hoping his voice sounded surly enough.

"That's what you told me the last time. Listen, we're both waiting for the same pigeon, why not be comfortable while we're at it?"

"I don't know what you're talking about, girlie," he said, slurring his words like he thought a bum should do. There was no chance of her recognizing him, he'd taken off all the shoe polish.

"Hey, what happened?" she asked, trying to get a look under his hat.

"What happened to your face? Last time I saw it, you were dark brown."

"I said get lost," he said. "You want trouble?"

"Goodness me, you're not going to do anything foolish right here in the middle of the street, are you? I mean, wouldn't it be better in some hallway, or down by the docks?"

He looked around. There were a lot of people on the street; it was a busy time, everybody was going into restaurants, bars, walking up and down. The streetlights were blazing. He knew all kinds of things happened, even in broad daylight, but he wasn't the type to do them.

He started walking away, hoping to give her the brush-off.

"Don't pretend you don't remember me," she said, coming after him. "The subway, a couple of quick ones in the ribs? You must remember that."

"I don't know nothing."

"I'm sort of hard to forget."

"Don't bother me."

"I won't bother you, I'll just keep you company."

"I'm minding my own business. I don't know nothing about no subway."

"Maybe it was your twin brother then, the one with the different color face. I see you wear the same clothes, you must be a gas when you're together."

When he stopped, she stopped. When he walked, she came with him.

"Look," he said, dropping the pretense of being a bum. "I don't know what you want, but just leave me alone."

"Want to call a cop? Want to put in a complaint?"

He said nothing. "That's what I thought. You know, we have a common interest, we could get along famously if you'd stop fighting it."

"Take my advice," he said. "Butt out. You might get hurt."

"Are you worried about that?"

"I don't want to see you get hurt."

"What about Baker Dilloway? Do you want to see him get hurt?"

"I don't know what you're talking about."

"Skinny kid, medium tall? Wears jeans with a love

patch on his behind. Lives over there. But I'm forgetting, you know where he lives, don't you?"

"Please," Abraham begged, "please go away and mind your own business."

"I have a feeling you're not what you pretend to be. I have a feeling you're not very happy. What's bothering you? Are you afraid of something?"

In all his life, he never met such a brazen person. Especially a girl. He didn't know what to make of her. What was her game? If she wasn't so young, he could almost believe she was a cop. But they wouldn't send a high school kid would they?

"Maybe we could help each other out," she was saying. She pulled him over to the side of the street. "If you're worried somebody might see you talking to me, I'll co-operate. But only if you do. You can pretend to give me the brush-off, real nasty like, see? And I'll meet you someplace where we can talk."

Abraham was completely befuddled. He wanted to protest, but he didn't know what he could say to her.

"And don't give me that I-don't-know-what-you're-talking-about routine again. What do you say? Look, I'm not interested in getting the cops in on this deal any more than you are. I'm sure you have your reasons and I have mine. You give me the big brush-off now and I'll meet you later. It's safe, believe me. You have to eat sometime, right? You come to this place like you're going to have a meal and I'll see you there."

She handed him a small white business card with the

name of a restaurant on it. When she saw him wavering she added, "A free meal in return for a short talk. That's all. No strings, nothing. You can only come out ahead."

"All right, all right," Abraham said. He didn't think anybody was watching, but he wouldn't put it past Grepp with all his angles. Besides, he wanted to find out what this crackpot knew. If he could nip it in the bud and save complications it would be to his benefit. Grepp wouldn't have to find out. He could take care of everything right at this end. If he could get her out of the picture, he would soon be on his way to Canada.

"When? In an hour?"

"Make it two," he said. Grepp couldn't expect him to spend the night on the street. He had to eat sometime. He had to take time off to go to the bathroom, take a nap. He wasn't superman.

He put the card in his pocket. Then he gave her a push. Perhaps it was overly harsh, but he wanted her to know that this wasn't kid stuff. He could be ruthless if necessary.

She took off and he breathed a sigh of relief. He took up his stance again, watching the kid's house, keeping an eye out for Gorshin, although it was possible he wouldn't recognize the man even if he fell over him.

Mary walked away. She was shaking and it surprised her to find out she was scared. Now she wasn't so sure it had been such a good idea after all.

She had decided to talk to him on the spur of the moment. There was no doubt about who he was, she recognized him instantly from the crazy hat and overcoat. She didn't have a plan, she just knew Baker was in some kind of trouble and she wanted to help him.

She had come home that afternoon feeling very uncertain about the whole thing. After two glasses of papaya juice and a couple of hours of getting nowhere with her thoughts, she looked up Baker's phone number and called. She made a promise with herself that if Baker were there, safe and sound, she would drop the subject and stop being nosy. The phone rang interminably but there was no answer. Unable to stay cooped up any longer, she went out for a walk and ended up at Sheridan Square. Her inclination was strongly in favor of walking down 10th Street toward Baker's house. But she figured another phone call wouldn't hurt. Better than barging in. She went into a phone booth and dialed. This time a woman answered. "Mrs. Dilloway?" she asked. "May I please speak to Baker?" She used her innocent schoolgirl voice. Mrs. Dilloway said Baker wasn't there and she sounded very upset. She started asking a lot of questions and Mary had to play dumb. Then to top it all off, a man got on. "Who's speaking, please? Who is this?" She hung up fast. She felt sure now that there was something fishy going on.

But she felt so helpless. She wanted to be careful and sensible, not fly off the handle. She didn't know the

155

whole story and even though it sounded bad, it might turn out to be nothing. She wanted to get the whole picture.

That's where Overcoat came in. He might be able to supply a few facts to help her decide what to do. No sense going to the police, if Baker's mother were really worried she would have done that already. Maybe the guy on the phone asking Who is this? was a cop.

And maybe Baker was mixed up in something the police shouldn't know about, at least from Baker's point of view. He wouldn't appreciate her calling the cops on him. She wanted to help him. Get him straightened out if she could. Pete would accuse her of playing psychiatrist again. But she felt sometimes like she had a vocation, or something. She couldn't turn her back. If she could get him out of a jam, help him go straight, it would be worth it. Maybe he was a pusher or a dealer, anything was possible. He could change. If the police got involved he would be arrested, the whole schmear. As soon as she saw Overcoat standing there across from the apartment, she knew she was going to do what she could on her own, without the cops. Good or bad, Overcoat was mixed up in it. The car that picked up Baker was the same one he had jumped into the other night.

She would play it by ear. First go back to the restaurant and tell Mario she was expecting company and she needed a table at the back, and to charge the spaghetti

156

to her. Mario was okay, he wouldn't blow it. She could count on him to be discreet and he wouldn't mention a thing to Pete if she told him not to. It was a good thing Monday was Pete's night off.

As she walked back to the restaurant she felt better than she had in weeks. She had something substantial now, something to do! School could wait. Pete would blow a gasket, but he would have to realize that she just wasn't going to make the scene at Carnegie Hall. It was her life. She had to live it the only way she knew how.

18

Baker was trussed up like a Thanksgiving turkey and stuffed face down on the floor of the car. He would have suffocated had it not been for the fact that his nose was pressed against the bottom of the door. The cold air that blew relentlessly into his nostrils smelled of gasoline. But at least it was air. He didn't know which was worse, the pain in his back and shoulders or the frost collecting in his sinuses.

There was no doubt that he had been captured. The question was, by whom? The men who had stuck the needle in his arm looked like men, but he couldn't be sure the Slynacks weren't behind it. He had come to a few minutes ago and there was no telling how long he was out. It seemed like days. And he had a headache, like a hangover. His mouth tasted fuzzy and sour. He thought of his mother's words that morning, a million light years away, "You'll have bad breath." Well, he had one hell of a case of bad breath now. He also had a terrible feeling that he'd wet his pants. Something was cold and damp down there.

At least they didn't put a gag in his mouth. He tried yelling when he woke up, it was an automatic reaction. His voice came out weak and muffled and he got dirt on his tongue. Whoever was in the front seat paid no attention to his helpless groans.

What could he do? He couldn't move, even to turn his head. He felt sick and miserable and not very inspired. No great solutions came to mind. He didn't even care. All he wanted to do was go home.

The car moved along remorselessly, like an infernal machine, disregarding his pain. Baker forced himself to try to get a grip on himself, forget his body and its misery and concentrate on what was happening. He had to listen for clues. He'd seen enough TV shows to know you could learn a lot even if you couldn't see. Blindfolded people were always hearing train whistles, voices, all kinds of noises which helped later on. Even smells could be significant, except that he couldn't smell anything but exhaust fumes. No wonder he had a headache. Didn't they care if he died back here?

Maybe they didn't. Slynacks would want only his body, they wouldn't care if he was dead.

Wait a minute, wait a minute, he told himself, first things first. It didn't necessarily have to be Slynacks. In fact, he was beginning to think the whole idea of Slynacks was just a figment of his imagination. For the time being, he must assume they were human, Homo sapien, flesh and blood, with all the limitations of men.

Above the roar of the tires, he heard a cough. Nothing more, no conversation. There had been two of them in the car and he assumed they were both in the front seat. Where were they taking him? And why?

He felt the car turn, go up an incline and then stop. The cold wind stopped blowing and the quiet was blissful. He tried to speak again.

"Hey," he croaked. "Hey."

He heard the door opening and someone getting out. Then the back door opened and he could see feet standing in front of him. Brown shoes with laces, he would remember that fact. They were scuffed at the toes and worn looking. A valuable clue.

"Want to get out and piss?" a voice asked him. Without waiting for an answer the person picked him up by the scruff of the neck and dragged him forward. He bumped his nose on the door. He was flung outward on to his feet and he stood only a moment before he collapsed. His legs were numb. There was a funny black curtain in front of his eyes.

"Come on, I don't have all day." Baker felt himself being lifted up again. He staggered forward, off balance because his hands were tied behind his back. He wanted to turn around and look at the man's face, but he was hurried forward toward some trees. They seemed to have pulled off into some woods. There were no other cars around.

"Take a leak, that's all, I don't have time for anything else."

Baker stood there wondering how he was going to unzip his pants.

"I don't have to," he said. He had wet his pants all right. He could see the stain.

"So why didn't you say so?" The man grabbed him again, this time Baker was faster, he swung around. He gasped.

Of course he realized it was a mask, he just hadn't been expecting it. One of those woolen ski hats that covered the whole face with openings for the nose and eyes. The effect was gruesome, the mask was purple with red trim around the eyeholes. The eyes that stared out were light blue and full of malice.

Light blue eyes, brown shoes, scuffed at the toes; Baker mentally stored these clues away in his mind. Not a very substantial set of facts, but facts nonetheless. He tried to envision the man's face as he had seen it earlier. Only a vague recollection of features came to mind, nothing he would be able to describe fully.

"Let's go," the man said.

"Where?" Baker asked. "What's going on?"

"Nothing to concern you. Just keep quiet, you won't get hurt." He started pushing Baker into the back, hurriedly, like he was afraid somebody might come along and see them.

"Not that way," Baker protested, "I can't breathe."

"Get in there, will you, I don't have time for arguments."

Baker resisted for only a second, he realized quickly that the man was much stronger than he was. With his hands tied, he had only his feet, and if he ran he would be caught again.

"Don't look for trouble," the man warned.

"Let me lie on my back," Baker asked. "Please," he added, politely.

"What do you think this is, a bed? Get in and shut up or I'll stuff your mouth for you." For a moment he seemed undecided. He pushed Baker down on the floor, head first, on his stomach again. Resting his foot on the small of Baker's back, he patted all his pockets, searching for something. He found it. "I better do it anyway," Baker heard him mumble to himself. "Now that you're awake there's a risk." He pulled Baker's chin up and Baker felt the cloth against his lips. "That'll keep you."

Baker began to swallow convulsively. He thought he was going to choke. I can't stand it, he thought, I can't stand it, I'm going to die.

But the car started up again and they were moving once more. Baker didn't die. The pain in his shoulders grew worse. His throat ached, his chest felt like lead, his nose refused to function. But he survived. He even slept, or rather he passed out from hyperventilation. He dreamed of Slynacks with long green arms. They were squeezing him, trying to get his insides out through his ears. He was aware of a change in the roadbed. Bumps, sharp jostles that slammed his head up and down on the floor.

When the car stopped and the motor died, he heard the sound of crickets. It was dark. The air that rasped through his stopped-up nose was fresh. They were in the country. He was dragged over dirt, grass, and his heel bumped on wooden steps. He felt as if his body no longer belonged to him, that he was only an outside observer watching a sack of potatoes being flung through a doorway. The bright lights blinded him. He had only a glimpse of bodies, inordinately long and thin.

"Slynacks," he managed to say before the curtain came down again, this time much darker and blacker than before.

"What did he say?" someone asked.

"Never mind, stick him on the cot."

He could hear their voices, he could feel them touching his body. But he couldn't see them.

"I'm blind," he thought without much concern. It didn't matter because he'd be dead soon, a hollow shell of a human body, to be used by the Slynacks when they went forth in the world of men.

"Don't forget to lock the door," he heard his mother say.

For some strange unknown reason, he started to cry.

19

Gorshin had been seeing the two cars in his rear-view mirror for a long time before it actually hit him. He was being followed! Christ, he thought, breaking out into an ice cold sweat, and he cursed himself for not being more careful. It had never occurred to him that someone would follow him out of Sawtruck. Maybe because he was remembering the battered old Volkswagen that had been parked in front of the old house for so long. He had subconsciously been watching for that and forgetting everything else.

He had to lose them, that was for sure, but how? For the time being, he could keep going while he figured it out. He could lead them around in circles. But eventually, he would have to make a move.

Now the problem was twofold. Before this, he had simply wondered where he was going to end up. He had not reached any decision and kept on heading southwest, vaguely intending to drive toward Chicago. He didn't know anybody in Chicago, but it was a big city, he could lose himself easily there. Now that plan would have to change, he had no intentions of being tailed all the way across the country. At any time, whenever he stopped for gas, food or whatever, they might make a move themselves and grab him. It was obvious they were organized. This time, they were planning to make no mistakes. Two cars. He wouldn't have a chance. He had to decide where to go and how to lose them.

He drove automatically, his mind racing. It was all so damn stupid. One little mistake in the lab, one overtired brain having a momentary lapse, sending the wrong signal to an equally tired, shaky hand. The hand picks up the wrong vial and boom, the human brain is drastically altered and all known facts become obsolete.

Of course it didn't happen all that simply. There were experiments, a lot of hours checking and rechecking results before he could believe it himself. He had been so naive. Making big plans, filled with excitement, planning to surprise Petersen with his discovery.

Gorshin's mind banked and went into a turn. He slipped back into the past and was once more the young white-coated technician, the underpaid lackey to Dr. Oswald Petersen, renowned autocrat of Waldsen Pharmaceuticals. They had been working on a variety of drugs that year and doing some farsighted experiments with d-lysergic acid diethylamide tartrate. Petersen could be brilliant, but he could also be pedantic. He was a hard taskmaster and this ambivalence in his personality created tension in the lab. Many of those who worked for him would have grabbed the chance to finesse him in any way they could. It became a general topic of conversational banter, how to outsmart the big man himself.

When Gorshin realized what he was on to, he knew it would be the chance for him. He couldn't wait to see Petersen's face when he demonstrated the effects of the new drug he had discovered. Poor old smug Petersen, always full of all the answers.

Gorshin worked secretly, staying on at the lab when everyone else went home. Petersen did not find this unusual, he admired hard work and encouraged his employees to overextend themselves whenever possible. They all thought he was brown-nosing for a raise in pay. They told him not to break his back. Gorshin let them rib him. He kept his secret.

Unfortunately, there was Felix. Felix Forbisher, human guinea pig, and the only other person who knew about Gorshin's experiments. He had needed somebody to work with and Felix had seemed like the ideal subject. He knew nothing about science, agreed to keep quiet and was interested only in cash.

It made for a nice working arrangement. Gorshin paid Felix out of his own pocket and Felix immediately spent his pay doing his favorite thing: drinking rum and Coke in the local poolroom. It was unlikely he would meet anyone from the lab in the poolroom and Gorshin felt confident that the experiments would be safely undercover until the big moment when he would shoot Petersen the results. At least that's what he thought.

But Felix wasn't quite so dull as he pretended to be.

166

Seeing a way to increase his assets, Felix made a few well-placed inquiries on the open market. He was under the impression Gorshin was developing a new hallucinogenic, something that would give all those tired, worn-out junkies a new high. By the time he realized his mistake, he was in too deep. Neither he nor Gorshin could stop the inevitable.

Gorshin remembered the momentous evening when he got the dosage correct at last. Felix was sitting in his usual place, bored and a little impatient. So far he had not experienced any thrills and he was losing the faith. Gorshin injected him with 50 micrograms of what Felix had nicknamed the Zinger because it was a less potent injection than the Zapper, the needle that Gorshin injected into his own arm as part of every experiment. Gorshin had explained to Felix that it was necessary for him to take the larger dosage because of the risk of dangerous side effects. It was for Felix's own protection, he explained. Felix accepted this, although with reservations. What Felix didn't know was that the recipient of the larger dosage was the only one who was going to experience anything at all. That's the way it was planned.

"How do you feel?" Gorshin had asked him a few minutes after administering the injection.

"Okay. Sort of dizzy. Maybe nauseous, you know?"

"That's all right, Felix, just relax, it will pass. Try not to move your head too quickly, and keep your eyes closed for a few minutes."

Gorshin himself was having a similar reaction. He turned the lamp aside and wrote his notes away from the bright light, which had begun to annoy his dilated pupils. He knew that both he and Felix would be feeling disturbance in the autonomic nervous system. There would also be somatic disturbances too, in the muscles. But all of this would pass very quickly and be replaced by the effects of Stage Two, the most important stage, in fact, the only important stage of the drug's effect. Stage Three would be the tapering off of the drug's potency and a gradual return to normal. Felix would feel nothing during Stage Two except a possible mild exhilaration. Gorshin would take the full effect of Stage Two alone. In a matter of ten or fifteen minutes he would begin to do what heretofore had been impossible. He would be able to read Felix Forbisher's mind.

They sat together in the locked lab. The silence was broken only by the soft murmur of the equipment and the scratch of Gorshin's pen. Then Felix started to twiddle his thumbs and clear his throat. He had opened his eyes, tested cautiously for more nausea, found he felt all right and immediately became bored. Gorshin, however, was growing more and more aware of Felix. Slowly, disconnected words touched his mind. They were Felix's words. Felix's thoughts. But they were in Gorsin's brain. It was like climbing inside of Felix. Or rather, like having Felix climb inside of him.

He knew it was a success this time. Before, he had felt the vague beginning of something, like hearing words

168

through a thick wall. He knew he was almost there, that only the dosage needed adjustment. Tonight, it happened. In less than half an hour, he found out everything he wanted to know. And more.

Felix Forbisher, believing that Gorshin had discovered a new drug that would give a bigger and better high than what was currently available on the open market, had secretly arranged a double cross. He was planning to get his hands on Gorshin's supply and sell out to the highest bidder. Only so far Felix had not experienced any highs and he was disappointed. He was getting restless. And worried, because he had made a lot of noise and promised delivery. He was getting mad.

"Sorry," Gorshin had told him when the drug began to wear off and he could no longer make contact with Felix's brain. "I guess we weren't very successful."

"Better luck next time," Felix said, eyes wary.

"There may not be a next time," Gorshin said, hoping to get Felix out of the picture altogether.

"Hey, listen, man," Felix broke in before Gorshin could explain that the experiments were over. "How come you're always having these downers, huh?" Rolling down his sleeve, he started to walk around the lab, handling things, asserting his presence. "Maybe you're not doing it right, you know? Maybe you should switch them needles around."

Too quickly, Gorshin said, "No, no that wouldn't work." The denial made Felix suspicious.

"It won't, huh? What exactly is supposed to happen?

169

I mean, when this thing hits the jackpot, what do we get out of it?"

"It's an antidote," Gorshin lied, thinking fast, "for the hallucinogens. Brings you back to reality. When it works, you find yourself thinking very clear. Straight and clear."

He hoped that Felix would be turned off by this explanation, but Felix looked thoughtful and he said, "Yeah, but you know something? I'm thinking pretty straight and clear right now. I think you're wrong, Doc, I think your experiment is a big success and you don't even know it."

Gorshin had underestimated Felix. He wasn't prepared for the blow on the head. Felix came up behind him and let him have it and then quickly prepared two needles and jabbed them home. And it was a credit to Felix that he performed the experiment exactly as he had seen Gorshin do it. With one exception: this time he gave himself the Zapper, and Gorshin was given the smaller dosage. Otherwise the outcome might have been very different for both of them. Gorshin wouldn't be running and Felix would be alive. But good old Felix had done it right and it had worked. He didn't get the psychedelic trip he had been planning on, but he got something else a hell of a lot bigger. The cat was out of the bag and howling.

Even so, when Gorshin came to he wasn't really worried. For one thing, Felix had used up the last of the drug and hadn't been able to find any more of it in the lab.

170

Also, Gorshin's notes were locked up, a precaution taken whenever Felix was present. He used only a sheet of paper for each session and wrote up the summary afterward. So Felix had nothing to take away with him that would give anyone else a clue to the nature of the drug, only his own experience. And nobody would believe Felix Forbisher when he told them he could read minds!

But somebody did. Because by the end of the month, Petersen had been murdered and Felix was missing and most likely dead. And Gorshin had been picked up on his way home one evening, forced into a car, blindfolded and taken to a dingy little room where an offer was made. Hand over the drug in exchange for money. When he said no thanks they upped the offer. He kept saying no until they believed him. Money wasn't going to buy it. Well, how about power?

Having learned his lesson with Felix, Gorshin did not make the mistake of underestimating these men. He quickly realized they were not the same breed of gangster he had seen depicted in the movies. They were dangerous fanatics with a cold-blooded and very serious plan to overthrow the government. Gorshin's formula would enable them to find out quickly and efficiently everything their victims were thinking. It was cheaper and more reliable than the usual methods of bugging and, what was worse, the victims would have no possible way of protecting themselves from it, and they might not even know it was happening. Eventually, no one would be

171

safe. They'd find a way to feed the drug into water supplies, food, ration it out so that they themselves would always be the readers while the rest of the world would be helplessly read.

He did not try to reason with them. But he knew they wouldn't kill him until they got what they wanted. Without Gorshin, there was no power, no nothing. And before they decided to threaten him with killing someone else, he had to act.

He told Clare what he had to do. He didn't know if she really believed him, it all sounded so fantastic. But the possible threat to Baker's life frightened her enough to agree to help him. He drove his car into the river one night, windows open, blood from his own purposely cut hand on the upholstery. He watched his wallet and credit cards float downstream like dead fish. Clare gave the cops a story of an unhappy and dissolving marriage. She was an actress, presumably she did a good job. At least they never involved her in any suspected foul play. He disappeared from her life. And from Baker's. He still didn't really know what she thought about it. When they saw each other, infrequently, they didn't talk about it. They were like old friends who have outgrown each other and have nothing left to say.

After so many safe years in Sawtruck, danger had seemed remote. When he first started visiting Clare and Baker, she was upset and afraid. She wouldn't let him come too often and insisted they stick to their original story that he was only a friend. It had been hard pretending to his son. He was often tempted to tell him, only he'd never been able to think of the right words to say. And as it turned out, Clare had been right. The danger was still there. It was better if Baker didn't know.

But he had no more time for daydreams about the past. He was being followed and he couldn't spend the rest of his life driving up and down the highway. He had to get them off his tail. More important, he had to find a new place to hide. But his brain was numb, and he had run out of ideas and solutions. Was it worth it to spend the rest of his life running? Charlie's death had discouraged him. Why not end it all? He should have stayed in Maine, put a bullet in his head in the comfort of his own home.

And then it came to him, beautifully simple. What better place to hide than his own house? If he could get back to Sawtruck without being followed, he might be safe. Because Sawtruck was the last place they would think to look for him. He'd have some breathing space, time to plan.

He knew what he had to do. Find a big public building with people inside of it. And make sure it had a men's room.

He swung off the highway at the next exit and started traveling the secondary roads which ran through the congested towns. It took another hour's driving before he found the perfect place.

Abandoning his car in the huge parking lot in front of a hospital complex, he raced toward a sign pointing to the

Out-Patient Department. Under his arm, he carried a can of talcum powder, a shaving mirror and an extra shirt.

Out of the corner of his eye he saw his pursuers turn into the lot. He hoped that a hospital would be a place just official enough to prevent their interfering right on the premises. And in a burst of creative inspiration, he cupped his free hand over his ear and screwed up his face in an imitation of pain.

Let them think he had an earache. Let them think what they liked just so long as they made the mistake of watching his car instead of him. If they did that, he could kiss them both goodbye. Because he had no intention of using the car again. He had other plans.

Half an hour later, a stooped gray-haired man emerged from the rear exit of the hospital. His back seemed slightly humped and he wore a drab brown overcoat that was too long in the sleeves. Blinking frequently, as if something irritated his eyes, he walked briskly toward a wide avenue beyond the hospital grounds. Stopping at an intersection, he lifted his hand to thumb a ride.

Moments later, he was picked up. He was smiling.

Meanwhile, around at the front of the hospital, two men in two separate cars grew bored, weary and belatedly nervous as they stared at Gorshin's car. After a time, hesitantly but not surprisingly, they began to stare at each other.

174

20

Before the sun came up on Tuesday morning, three things happened:

Abraham confessed to Mary the Hulk, under duress and with the help of several plates of fettucine, which he had never been able to resist. His confession, he hoped, would relieve him of the guilt. It was a long shot he was willing to take to get out of the whole mess and save his neck. Still not convinced she was no policewoman in disguise, he made a deal that he would take her to the place they were holding Baker. That's all. It was up to her then, she could call the cops if she liked, but he was getting out of it. He could go away with a clear conscience and empty pockets. Whichever way he looked at it, he was going to lose.

John Bones arrived back in Sawtruck, and not far behind him came Gorshin. Bones went straight to Doc Pepper's house, feeling lousy, tired and frustrated and not a little concerned for Doc's reputation. He knew Doc shouldn't have acted on his own in the first place and now they had lost Gorshin besides. Gorshin himself stumbled through the thick underbrush of the woods behind Old Tavern Road. He was still dressed in the stolen overcoat and his hair was still grayed by the talcum powder, but he had long since discarded the hump he had made out of the crumpled shirt. He was anxious to get inside the house before daybreak, yet he had to move slowly and cautiously if his plan was going to work. There were only a few birds awake to watch his progress. But below the surface of the earth, something sensed, or perhaps smelled, his coming.

The telephone rang in the Dilloway apartment and the first contact with the kidnappers was made. At least that's what Clare Dilloway and Katz hoped. It was a short and disjointed conversation and left them no wiser than before.

"Mrs. Dilloway?" a voice had asked her. "Put your husband on the phone."

"What? I don't have . . ." she started to say, but the voice broke in, "No lies, please."

"I have no husband," she insisted, much to Katz's dismay.

"We want to talk to George Gorshin," the voice said, and it was a statement of fact, irrefutable.

"He's not here," Clare said.

"When he comes, tell him to wait by the phone." That's all, no threats, no instructions. Nothing.

"Do you think he will come here?" Katz asked her when she put down the phone.

"I don't know," was all she could say.

They had already tried Gorshin's number in Sawtruck and then Katz had checked with Larry Pepperpot, the local police chief, who was supposed to have been keeping an eye on Gorshin's whereabouts for the past ten years. Katz didn't tell Mrs. Dilloway that Doc Pepper had fouled up the works trying to run the show his own way and do Gorshin a favor at the same time. Of course Doc had no way of knowing that Gorshin's trip was going to come at the same time his son had been kidnapped. "I was trying to do the poor fellow a good turn," Doc said. "Seemed so pointless, hiding up here in the hills, his wife and family so far away." Doc had been lulled into a false sense of security, almost forgetting why he had been asked to keep tabs on Gorshin in the first place. "He was acting nervous, so I told him to take a vacation. Thought he'd go down to New York and see his kid." He didn't say so, but Katz knew Doc had always hoped to make a big splash sometime. He'd sent a man to tail Gorshin, just in case, just to make sure he was going to New York. Then he'd done some investigating and realized his mistake. Gorshin had cleared out. "Thought he was going to give up this nonsense," Doc said. "Go back home again where he belonged." Doc was apologetic, he had a few irons in the fire, he said. He was going to check up on a few things and he'd let them know. Katz didn't have much faith.

"I can't believe everybody knew," Mrs. Dilloway kept saying. "All this time you all knew George was alive while

177

we were pretending. Stupidly keeping up this idiotic act for Baker's safety."

"Your son was always the only possible target," Katz explained. "We knew they might try to get to your husband through him."

"But all these years, why let it go on and on?"

That was a good question, Katz thought, but then it really wasn't the FBI's business if George Gorshin wanted to give up his wife and kid. For all he knew, it might have been a way to cop out on the marriage, who knew what people did for private reasons? All they could do was wait, and until now they hadn't had much hope in the waiting.

"They won't give up," Felix Forbisher had told the FBI, singing his song in return for amnesty and a Dynel wig. "You mark my words, you know what I mean? Maybe not next week, next month, even next year. But sooner or later. Take it from me." Felix had been cut up pretty bad, almost killed. But nobody really believed what he said. They figured Gorshin had a commodity, a drug, that someone wanted enough to kill for, but they never believed in the mind-reading act. Gorshin had been scared enough to rig a phony death scene and go into hiding. As long as there was a possibility he would be contacted again, and they could nab Petersen's murderer, they were willing to watch. And Felix had been right after all. Not sooner. But later.

"Come on, Mrs. Dilloway, why don't you lie down,"

Katz said to her. "Try to get some sleep." He made her go to the bedroom. He felt sorry for her, but he didn't know what else he could say. They had a long hard wait ahead of them.

He tiptoed down the hall to Baker's bedroom. He had been in the kid's room once before, long ago when he was fresh on the job and very enthusiastic. In return for his enthusiasm he had been hit on the head by a can of stewed tomatoes which came crashing down when he opened the door. When he had his wits back together again he saw that the whole room was booby-trapped, and it had taken him a hell of a time to reset the trap. He never went back, preferring to keep an eye on the kid from afar.

Now he entered the room cautiously. No flying canned goods this time, but a terrible smell of garlic instead. There was garlic putty all over the window and more of it around the desk drawers. Either Baker Dilloway was scared stiff of vampires or it was some new religion. Katz pulled the stuff off the desk and pried the lock with a screwdriver. The top drawer contained the usual junk, pencils, papers, a regular mess. But in the second drawer he hit the jackpot. There were maps and notebooks listing addresses of offices and apartment buildings the kid seemed to have been casing. What for? A teen-age housebreaker? Underneath the notebooks was a thick leather-bound diary with a lock on it. Katz had no compunction about breaking it. Inside were entries, all of them cryptic, about something called Slynack activities. At first Katz thought it was some kind of club or political organization, but the more he read, the less sure he was. If the kid's father supposedly could read minds, what was so unusual about some stringy beings who came from outer space and were preparing to take over the world?

The shrill ringing of the doorbell brought him back to reality. He raced to the door, colliding with Clare Dilloway in the hall. She was hoping it was Baker, no doubt, but Katz knew it was only the men bringing the equipment for the phone. When he let them in he wondered if Lil might be peering out of her apartment, wanting to know what was going on. In a little while he would have to go downstairs and be Katz the Janitor again. Katz the FBI man didn't stand a chance, but a janitor could find out plenty. Like the walls, he could be standing there without being seen.

Besides, they needed heat and hot water and there was nobody going to give it to them except Katz. Lil was really going to miss him when this was all over.

21

He heard them talking, all the time, they never shut up. The old one picked on the long skinny one. Farn was the skinny one's name and he was always doing everything wrong. Old Grepp nagged and if he wasn't nagging he was telling everybody how great he was. Baker hated his guts. He hated the skinny one's guts too, but he couldn't help feeling sorry for him once in a while. He tried to get on Farn's good side, hoping to bribe him. But that was a laugh. What did he have to bribe anybody with? And anyway, Farn had his moments when he acted very peculiar, so he really couldn't be trusted anymore than Grepp could.

The first night was the worst, he kept waking up and expecting to find himself in his own bed at home. Every time he woke up he had to relive the whole thing all over again, telling himself it was no dream, it was real. The next morning he felt very sick. He couldn't remember ever feeling so sick in his whole life. "I'm dying," he told them when they came into the room. They stood next to the cot, looking down at him like he was some kind of bug or bad joke. They both had big yellow teeth and long, stretched faces, the skin pulled back tight over

181

the bones. One was tall with extremely rounded shoulders. The other one was shorter and wider with strangely shiny white hair that stuck straight out over his forehead. They didn't sympathize. "Give him some water," the white-haired one said. "Oh yes, Grepp," the skinny one replied and simpered away to get it. He brought back some flat warm water in a paper cup. Baker was so thirsty he drank it down fast without worrying if it was drugged or poisoned. Then they untied his hands and feet and let him get up from the cot.

"Walk around, move your legs," Grepp ordered. And as he walked in circles around the room, they watched him, studying every movement so closely that Baker felt surer than ever they were Slynacks studying an earthling specimen for future use.

But later, after he had taken a leak into a tin can provided for that purpose and had eaten a bowl of gluey oatmeal that stuck to the roof of his mouth, he suddenly felt better. He heard the two of them talking and moving around as if everything were normal, and there was also the very comforting aroma of percolating coffee drifting in to revive his mind. No more Slynacks, he decided. He would consider them mortal and deal with them as men. It was the only rational approach and the only way to keep his sanity. With men he had a chance. With Slynacks there was no hope at all.

When he wasn't eating or using the tin can or walking the regulation ten times around the room, Baker was tied up on the cot and had a strip of tape sealing his mouth. Lying on his back, all he could do was look up at the ceiling or to the left or right and he had plenty of time to study the room. The ceiling was peeling, the walls full of nails and square marks where pictures had once hung on the faded wallpaper. The room contained a chest of drawers with missing knobs, and mildew growing on it, a fairly new-looking chair and a lamp table. There was also a bookcase, lopsided and packed with mouldy books. The window was covered over with a blanket and the floor was covered with a mothy old Oriental rug full of holes. But on top of the dresser there was a comb, brush and mirror set and some bottles of what looked like perfume. Hanging on the back of the door was a yellow bathrobe, long, with lace on the sleeves. Someone had tried to make the room look lived-in, without much success.

Sort of adjusting to the situation, and because there was nothing else he could do, Baker lay on the cot, dreaming and dozing and smelling the good smell of the coffee, which helped to cover up the dank mustiness of the room and his own sweat.

But in the middle of the afternoon there was some kind of disturbance. He woke up to the sound of Grepp's voice, excitedly giving orders to Farn.

"The closet, don't just stand there with your mouth open. Move!"

"Yes, Grepp, yes," Farn fluttered and clucked, and he

183

came springing into the room to yank Baker off the cot.

The closet into which Farn, with surprising strength, flung Baker was actually a crawl space under the eaves. The entry was through a real closet and the opening was concealed by a piece of wallboard and the junk which was stored in the closet. Crumpled in the dark, Baker heard Farn pushing the boxes and stacks of old magazines against the makeshift door of his hiding place. Then the door of the closet was shut and he could hear no more from the room. But he heard a car outside the house. And the slamming of car doors. He could see nothing except small pinpricks of light where the roof leaked. He hoped they wouldn't leave him there for a long time. Compared to this, the cot was luxury.

There was a low rumble of voices and then, quite clearly, Baker heard the word, "Gorshin." I'm dreaming, he thought, it's only wishful thinking. There was some laughter and muttering. More doors and the car started up and went away.

It seemed like a hundred years before Farn came back. He pulled Baker out by his feet and dumped him back on the cot. When Baker turned over and saw Farn's face he sucked his breath involuntarily with fear. Farn's long yellow teeth, always so prominent in his taut face, were covered with what looked like blood. The thin lips were stained with it and some was smeared on the chin. Farn looked at him quizzically. "What's wrong?" he asked.

But before Baker could answer, Grepp was in the

room, nagging again. "What's taking so long, Farn?" He came closer. "Look at yourself, Farn, you better get cleaned up." Grepp did not seem shocked, only disgusted.

"Yes, Grepp," Farn said humbly. But he hung back until Grepp left the room.

"I'll give you some cheese," he whispered to Baker, leaning over confidentially, his bloodstained lips uncomfortably near. Baker flinched and turned his head away. "What's wrong?" Farn asked, straightening up and looking offended. "I meant to be kind," he whispered indignantly as he checked over his shoulder to make sure Grepp wasn't listening. "It's only cheese, nothing else. I wouldn't play a joke on you." Some suspicion crossed his mind and he added, "Nothing dirty either," gory lips suddenly prim.

"Farn! Come out of there," Grepp called.

Farn turned and fled.

Not Slynacks, Baker thought, struggling to maintain reason, but maybe not men either. He racked his brains for possible explanations for Farn's strange appearance. He tried not to succumb to ridiculous notions like vampires. The only trouble was, if he could have believed in Slynacks, why not a simple old-fashioned thing like vampires?

He promised himself he wouldn't eat the cheese or anything else they gave him. But when Farn brought supper, pathetically arranged on a tray in an attempt to

185

appear inviting, his face was clean. The blood was gone and Baker was hungry. Too hungry to care if they were feeding him arsenic or strychnine. He ate the dry cheese, which had traces of blue mold on it, and managed to swallow most of the inevitable and sticky oatmeal. In addition to this generous repast, Farn gave him a paper cup of milk. It was powdered milk made with the same warm water he had tasted earlier.

"Thanks, that was nauseating," he told Farn, who was hovering over him, waiting to take back the tray.

"No need to be nasty," Farn said. He snatched the tray away and began to bind Baker's wrists. "I don't like to do this," he said. But he pulled the knots tight and went away with a smile on his face.

Where are the boys? Baker thought. Why don't they get their asses over here? A couple of blasts from the fire stick and those two jokers would be splat paste. Duck soup. A cinch. Oh christ, I'm not going to bawl again. Where are you? Where is anybody? Why don't you get over here and dust them off, get me out of here? Mr. Big needs help.

Nobody came. Baker started to dream about onions. He could smell them, french fried onions, fat brown rings, burning on the edges. Ketchup, mustard, succotash. He started to laugh. He hated succotash.

Dear Gorshin, why don't you rescue me? I've been writing you but you never answer. Sincerely Yours, Baker Dilloway.

He kept on laughing until he fell asleep

"Listen," Farn said, face gloomily concerned. "I don't think he's feeling well."

"He's fine," Grepp said. "He's a kid, kids are strong, they can take it. Besides, it takes a long time to die."

"I'm worried," Farn said.

"I'm not," Grepp said.

Grepp was not really worried, but he was not exactly pleased that the police had come this afternoon. On the other hand, it had gone all right and maybe it was better this way. The fat policeman had been satisfied that only Mr. Smith and his bedridden wife lived in the house. What could two old codgers do to anyone? Mrs. Smith was there plain as day had the police wanted to see for themselves. It was a lucky thing that they didn't, however, because Grepp wasn't sure that Farn, dressed and made-up like a woman, was exactly convincing. But Grepp himself played his part admirably, as a harmless, slightly eccentric nobody. And if he and his wife wanted to live in a shambles it was their own business, they had paid the rent in advance.

"Don't look so glum," he told Farn encouragingly. "They were only looking for Gorshin. It's logical they should ask here since we're his neighbors."

Farn slouched toward the kitchen with the dirty dishes. He was feeling glum in spite of Grepp's sales talk. He knew things weren't going the way Grepp had planned. Gorshin had disappeared and they didn't know where he was. Klinc had lost him early in the game and worse still, he had been spotted by someone who looked a lot like the police chief's sidekick, Bones. To be on the safe side, Grepp sent Klinc to Florida. So much for Klinc, but Grepp was upset. What was this Bones doing all the way down near Boston?

Then there was Abraham; Grepp couldn't make contact with him. Loose ends were piling up. Grepp sent Boris back to New York to find out what was going on. Which meant they had nobody up here with them now, just the two of them alone. With Gorshin's son and Gorshin's dog. Farn didn't know which one of them caused him more grief, the dog or the boy. He didn't like to see them tied up, it went against him. That's why he didn't tell Grepp that the dog had chewed through the rope. What could happen, the dog would walk around and get a little exercise. He couldn't escape from the tunnel. "Be careful," Farn had told him, "don't let Grepp know you're off that rope." He could almost swear the dog understood. And he hadn't tied him up again.

But with the boy it was different. Grepp would notice right away if he untied the boy. All Farn could do was try to make things a little easier for him, giving him some extra food and whatnot. If it were up to Grepp, the poor kid wouldn't even have a pot to piss in. He just hoped they wouldn't have to kill him. He wouldn't like that at all. But when he got right down to it, Farn had to admit he felt worse about the dog. Somehow it just wasn't as sad when it came to killing humans.

He put the tray down on the kitchen table and threw the paper cup away. The oatmeal bowl had to be rinsed out with stale, leftover soapy water. The house had no running water, no faucets, no toilets, nothing. The tin sink in the kitchen had no drain, what good was it? They used bottled water and Farn had to bail out the sink and Grepp said it was no problem, but what did he know about problems? He just gave the orders, he didn't have to wash dishes.

Feeling grouchy, Farn clattered around and Grepp reprimanded, "Shut up. I can't hear myself think."

Grepp was thinking hard. There was a great big lapse in operations and it was staring him in the face. What good was the kid without his father? And how were they going to find the father? They couldn't exactly advertise. They couldn't even go out looking with this reduction in personnel. Now that Boris was down in New York, he couldn't even get the phone calls made.

Grepp felt like throwing in the rag. To go on with operations he needed to get in touch with the Top, tell him they needed more men. But the Top was strict on security, had warned, "Don't call me, I'll call you." Grepp suspected the Top might not be all he cracked himself up to be. In any case, he no longer really cared about the Top. All he could do was wait.

But since waiting was essentially boring, Grepp found himself nodding in his chair, lulled by the scratch of Farn's broom. Had he been feeling more like himself, he would have heard even the slightest sound outside the house almost before it started. But Farn's sweeping had hypnotized his discouraged ears and only when the

189

broom stopped did Grepp notice something amiss. Lurching into action, he raced up the steep staircase to where Baker Dilloway was supposedly lying bound and gagged. He hoped it wouldn't be too late, that the kid had not already jumped out the window. Farn was coming up hotly behind him and when Grepp opened the door and saw, against all expectations, that Baker was still on the cot, hands and feet tied, he stopped short in surprise. Farn crashed into him, shrieking with alarm and pain.

"Stop the noise," Grepp demanded. He listened. Definitely. Someone outside the window. Motioning for Farn to dispose of Baker as quickly as possible, Grepp crept back downstairs and let himself out of the house. He noiselessly made his way around to the side. There in the moonless dark, two figures were attempting to climb the ancient trellis with the aid of nothing more than a pencil flashlight. One of the figures, wide and curiously top-heavy, was halfway up the wooden frame which was creaking and leaning precariously away from the wall.

Normally Grepp would not have been unduly concerned over facing two possible intruders because he knew the weapon he always carried, just as if it were part of his anatomy, was silent, swift and clean. Unfortunately, he could not clearly see who his enemies were. He did not want to risk shooting an important personage like the Sawtruck police chief. So instead of taking the offensive, he cleared his throat and asked, mildly distraught, "What are you doing?" He felt this would be a logical question for an innocent elderly householder to ask. No cop was going to trap him acting out of character!

There was a momentary startled silence. Then one of the figures disengaged itself from the other and came toward Grepp. "Grepp?" it asked in a tremulous voice. Not waiting for an answer, it ran back and began to pull the other figure off the wall.

"Hey, wait, hey, what's the matter with you?" the top-heavy climber shouted and came down with a crash, bringing most of the trellis down too. "Oh my leg, oooooh, damn, what did you do that for? Are you crazy?"

"Don't move, I got you covered," the other one threatened, and Grepp saw that it was Abraham.

"What are you talking about? Stop the clowning around, will you? Help me up. I think I broke my ankle, damn it." It sounded like a girl.

"Stay where you are," Abraham said and he turned to Grepp. "Here she is," he offered.

"Here who is?" Grepp asked. At the sound of his voice, the girl froze.

"I brought her, I had to. She's dangerous. She knows too much." Abraham was breathing fast and his hands were shaking. They were also empty, he didn't have a gun.

"You brought her? Here?" Grepp asked, incredulous.

The girl remained in a heap on the ground. Grepp could now see that what had made her seem top-heavy was a knapsack strapped to her back. She screamed.

"Double-crosser, stinking double-crosser!" Trying to get up from under the weight of the knapsack and trellis, she clawed the air toward Abraham.

"Bring her inside," Grepp said. His voice was cold and calm. Abraham struggled to get the girl to her feet. She screamed and beat him off. At last Farn came out to help. They pulled her across the unkempt lawn and into the house. Farn helped her get the knapsack off her back. She hit him on the chin for his trouble.

"Get away," she said. "Let me get my hands on that piece of shit over there."

Abraham stepped back, white in the face.

"If you will restrain the young lady," Grepp said to Farn, "Abraham and I will have a private talk."

"I'm the one you want to talk to," the girl shouted. "Ask me first. He didn't bring me up here for the reason he says he did. He brought me up here to help him."

"Help him do what?" Farn asked as he wound the rope.

"Help him rescue Baker."

Farn opened his mouth to say something, but a stern look from Grepp made him close it.

"Baker?" Grepp asked.

"Baker Dilloway. Never heard of him, right?"

"Can't say I have," Grepp replied. He was pushing Abraham to another room. When he got him there he shoved him inside and slammed the door, leaving Farn and the girl alone.

"So, who are you?" she asked Farn in a conversational tone.

Farn kept winding the rope, afraid to say something Grepp wouldn't like.

"Good guys or bad guys?" she asked. He didn't answer.

"Would you mind taking my boot off before you tie me up? I think my ankle's swollen."

Obligingly, Farn unzipped the boot and eased it off. He poked at the swelling and pulled at her toes. "Only a sprain," he said.

She watched him a moment and said, "Do you have a thing about toes?"

Farn raised a quizzical eyebrow. "I can see you're definitely a toe man," she said and pulled her foot away from him.

Grepp came back. "Take her upstairs," he said. "Abraham will help you. I think for the time being we will keep them both hidden. It's safer that way."

"Both?" Farn asked, hesitating.

"Yes both. It doesn't matter to mention it, Farn. Thanks to Abraham, this Hulk person knows the boy is here."

"Miss Hulk to you," she said.

"But I mean," said Farn, "should I put them together?"

"There's no harm in it, Farn. They'll be tied up."

193

Abraham snorted but Farn blushed. "I didn't mean that, Grepp. What I meant was . . ."

"Never mind what you meant," Grepp snapped. His patience was wearing very thin. "Get her up there."

To make up for his previous blunders, Abraham grabbed her arms roughly, yanked her to her feet and pulled her toward the stairs.

"I can walk," Mary said. "On my own two feet. Just keep your slimy hands off me!" She had one boot on and one off and nobody seemed to be noticing.

"Put a gag in her mouth," Grepp said. "Shut her up."

Farn led the way, thinking Was it never going to end? He envisioned the attic full of bodies, all of them tied up like rolled roasts, all of them stuffed under the eaves of the house, getting mouldy like the cheese. He put a gag on her mouth the way Grepp told him to. But it was cloth instead of tape and he didn't tie it as tightly as he might have. He pulled the magazines and boxes away from the opening at the back of the closet and shined a flashlight in. Baker, bent in half against the roof, blinked.

"A surprise," Farn said, not feeling very funny. "Some-one to keep you company."

They pushed the heavy, uncooperative body through the hole. She came through lopsided, landing with her head away from Baker's face and her feet in his lap. The door was closed and they were plunged into darkness.

"Hmmm, ummm," Mary gurgled behind the gag.

194

But Baker was too flabbergasted to try to mumble in return. He couldn't see and he couldn't ask, but he had a terrible horrible feeling that this body they had shoved in with him was none other than Mary.

She kept moving around and every time she did, her foot pressed painfully into a delicate place in his groin. He heard her making sounds, rasping and slurping. Then her feet came off his lap and like a fulminating whale, she turned herself the other way around, her head landing where her feet had been.

He froze, shocked to find her nose where her toes had been. But she didn't stay there long, she prodded and pushed and probed until he realized she wanted him to help her get her face near his hands which were tied behind his back. Snorting and snuffling, she managed to get his fingers hooked into the piece of cloth around her mouth. He worked at it, getting bitten in the process, and at last the gag came off.

"Oh, thank you," she cried, testing her lips, "I thought I was going to die of claustrophobia."

"Mmmmmmmmm," he said.

"That Abraham's a mother," she hissed.

"Hmmmmmmmm," he said.

"Listen, I have good news," she rattled on. "They don't look too smart down there. Weird but not clever. We'll be out of here in no time."

"Ummmmmmmm," he said, getting desperate.

"But I have to take a rest first. I have to relax a

minute. I've been running around all day and on top of that I fell off the house and sprained my ankle. I've got to get some sleep."

She rolled herself over on to his lap again, nose up this time.

"Ymmmmmmm," he said, running out of saliva.

"It's all right," she said sleepily. "Don't worry. Everything's all right."

After a few moments he heard, although he couldn't believe it, her snore.

22

Gorshin spent almost all day sleeping. He had intended to take a short nap, but when he woke up it was late afternoon and someone was walking around outside. Immediately, he realized how careless he had been. He had automatically gone upstairs to his own bed and collapsed on it. Now he was trapped on the second floor with no place to hide but the proverbial closet. He went to the window but didn't risk even taking the slightest peek out of it. Instead he strained his ears, hoping to hear who was outside. Luckily, he had relocked the back door through which he had come early that morning. And he didn't think there were any telltale signs around, he had worn the overcoat to bed because the house was so cold. But if they came upstairs they might notice the bed, and see the talcum powder which had rubbed off onto the bedspread.

Someone seemed to be making his way around the house, as if checking the windows and doors and trying to see inside. In a few moments, he heard two voices under the bedroom window. Doc Pepper's drawl was easily recognized. Bones was with him. They were agreeing on something, because Bones kept saying "Ayuh,

197

Ayuh," in his laconic way. He stayed perfectly still, afraid even the slightest movement might cast a shadow that would catch Doc's eagle eye. At last he heard them drive away.

He wouldn't risk such a mistake again. From now on he would have to live in hiding within his own house, keeping away from the windows, not turning lights on after dark. A miserable existence, but it would give him time to think and plan, something he would not be able to do while running.

He had enough food to last him. He could turn the water pump on in the early morning hours, then shut it off again once the tank was filled. He could even risk using the stove once in a while if he had to. The kitchen would be safe because it faced a wide open space of grass and garden at the back of the house. The windows were high up and anybody approaching would be seen before they could see him. It had the extra advantage of being next to the cellar door and this was important because he planned to do most of his thinking, and sleeping, down there. So long as nobody actually knew he was in the house, he'd be relatively safe hidden among the tarps and tin cans. All those survival supplies were going to come in handy at last.

He had it all planned and yet, when he heard Doc's car going down the driveway, he was almost tempted to run out after it. Which brought him to the reasons why he had not gone to the police at the start. He'd been scared, of course. But he also had had a nasty suspicion that as many people would want to exploit his secret in the name of peace as wanted it for less savory reasons. It was a very exploitable secret. And a much better method for extracting information than any of the other known drugs. It could be used so quietly, so simply on an unguarded mind. Operating as usual, the mind would never suspect it was being sucked dry.

The privacy of the mind was the only retreat left. Invading that privacy, at any cost, was wrong. Gorshin could see that now. He had been wrong to experiment even on Felix Forbisher. Unfortunately, the damage was done. He had no idea how to undo it except by eliminating himself.

The trouble was, he didn't want to die.

But he might just as well be dead and buried, he thought when he went down to investigate his new quarters in the cellar. With the upstairs door shut and the flashlight off, it was exactly like a grave. Arming himself with spare batteries and a couple of cans of cold chili, he settled in a corner with the flashlight on, not wanting to be in total darkness yet, afraid to smoke in case Doc Pepper decided to come back and might smell the pipe.

He was contemplating the reasons for Doc's visit when he heard the whine. It made him jump and drop the flashlight which went out. He spent a few nervous moments feeling around on the cold floor, afraid of touching something unknown and horrible. He found the light, put it on again and sat back, almost daring the sound to repeat itself. It did. And he was no better prepared for it because he jumped out of his skin again, only this time he held on to the light.

Well, it sounds like a dog, he said to himself, and it didn't make him feel better because he immediately thought of Charlie and Charlie's dog-ghost coming back to haunt the cellar.

The whines were getting furious, with an occasional yip thrown in for good measure. Gorshin, in a fit of reason, decided they must be real, not ghostly. He began to search. A certain muffled quality about the noise made him think of crevices or holes in the walls and he pushed a few large tin barrels of civil defense toilet paper out of the way, searching the walls behind him. But only a few moments of looking made him realize the sounds were coming from underneath the cellar floor. Which should have been impossible because as far as he knew, there was nothing underneath the cellar except dirt and rock, all the way down to the core.

But, feeling insanely reasonable, he decided to accept this impossibility and began to clear the floor. When the barrels and boxes were out of the way, he got down on his hands and knees and inspected the floor with the aid of the inadequate flashlight. It almost missed some rectangular grooves which looked very possibly like a trap door. He felt his skin crawl. It was frightening enough to think of how such a door might have been cut into the cement, but it was even more frightening to think of what he might find underneath it.

The whines had ceased now, as if the creature were waiting patiently for him to open the door. He had no idea how to open it. The blade of his penknife snapped when he tried to pry it. There was no latch or handhold. But when he used a small crowbar, the door came up effortlessly and he realized he had been expecting it to be much heavier.

Immediately the whines were renewed, excited and loud. Setting the slab aside, Gorshin looked down into a black hole, his flashlight illuminating the sad, worn but very recognizable face of Charlie. Without considering consequences, Gorshin leaned down and pulled the dog up.

He was very dirty and lean and did not smell his usual appealing self, but Gorshin could have cared less. Only after much tail wagging, paw shaking and mutual slobbering did he stop to think of the danger. Then he went back and looked into the hole again and saw the tunnel.

It all fell into place: the appearance of the Smiths next door, the sound of locomotives, Charlie's sudden disappearance. He sat back on his heels and Charlie, as if sensing the necessity, tried to jump back down into the hole. Gorshin hoped he understood just how necessary it was for him to go back again. Because one thing was for sure, Charlie didn't dig the tunnel or put him-

201

self into it. Whatever had would find him missing and come looking. But if there was any looking to be done, Gorshin wanted to be the one to do it.

Checking to see that the cover wouldn't fall accidentally back into place, Gorshin lowered himself down after Charlie. It was very dark and he was sorely tempted to use the flashlight, but he cautiously allowed Charlie to lead him instead. Like walking down a long nightmare, Gorshin felt his heart pounding and his knees shaking. At the end of the tunnel was a faint light. It seemed as if he would never reach it.

23

They were propped up, side by side, like two oversized dolls who had been thrown into the attic, no longer wanted. The attic was cold but they kept each other warm. Warm enough for Baker to smell his own rancid sweat trickling down inside his dirty shirt. Mary was awake after her nap, scratching an itch on her nose by rubbing it along his sleeve. It was very intimate, but Baker never felt less turned on. The excitement of her presence had worn off and he almost wished he were alone again.

"I have to go to the bathroom," she said. "What should I do? Shout?"

Baker shook his head and made sounds behind the tape on his mouth.

"I can't understand a word you're saying. Wait a minute, maybe I can get that damn tape off."

He felt her face close to his and saw the glint of bared teeth. With vampires still on his brain, he couldn't help recoiling.

"Come on, cooperate," she said and scraped her mouth against his, trying to get her teeth under the edges of the tape. With much slurping and a lot of her saliva slopping down his chin, she succeeded. Catching the end of the tape, she pulled, freeing his lips inch by pain-ful puckering inch.

"What a relief," he croaked. "Thanks."

"Now at least we can talk," she said. She was talking too loud.

He shushed her. "Keep it down, they'll hear you."

"But I have to pee," she said. "I'll have to call them. Very soon."

"And they'll put the tape back on again, and your gag. Can't you wait? Besides, I don't really think you're going to like the facilities."

"Why?"

"It's a tin can, in the bedroom. I've been constipated since I got here."

"Anal retentive," Mary said. "I don't have those problems." But she sounded less than pleased with the arrangements. "They must have a bathroom for them-selves."

"Who knows? Maybe they don't need one."

"What do you mean?"

"Never mind," Baker said, testily. He wasn't going to allow himself to start thinking Slynacks again.

"Well, you don't have to get so annoyed. It's a fact of nature, after all. I can't help it if I'm not able to whip it out like you can and pee down through the floorboards. It's useful, having a penis. Women's Lib wouldn't agree, but I always thought it came in handy for things like convenience-in-peeing."

204

"Christ."

"Did you ever notice," Mary went on, ignoring him, "how in the movies people never have to go to the bathroom? They get trapped in elevators and down in subways and they never wet their pants."

"Do you mind if I change the subject?" Baker asked.

"That happened to Pete once, he almost got mugged and he wet his pants. He didn't know until he got home."

"Would you mind telling me what you're doing here?"

"Pete's my father." She stopped. "Sorry, what were you saying?"

Baker found that having his hands tied made him nervous. He wanted to use his hands, wave them around, make gestures when he talked. He thumped them on the eaves behind him. "You. What are you doing here?"

"What are you?"

There was a moment of silence as they glared at one another, Baker exasperated, Mary annoyed and trying to get her glasses back on straight by wrinkling her nose. Neither one of them could see the other clearly in the dark.

"I asked you first," Baker said weakly. He had only just realized the full impact of her question. What the hell was he doing here?

"I don't suppose it matters now if I tell you I saw you getting into that car outside your school . . . that was your school, wasn't it? Listen, I was not following you,

205

you understand, not after you got so uptight about it, but I just happened to be going that way myself. So anyway I saw this car that looked like another car I had once seen and it all looked fishy to me, but Pete, that's my old man, he's always telling me to stop playing Miss Psychiatrist and do I think I'm going to save the world, so I didn't do anything right away, you know? But I thought about it and the more I thought, the more I was sure something was wrong. Then when I caught Abraham the Double-crosser watching your house, I knew something was up."

"Abraham?"

"Yeah, he told me what happened and brought me up here. You know, he was the one with the overcoat on that I saw in the subway following you. We made a deal for him to bring me up here. At first he didn't want to come with me, but he's no good at directions and anyhow I wasn't going to hitchhike alone. He was going to help me, he said. But as soon as he saw his pals he turned me over to them."

"Did you call the police?" Baker asked. "Or anything like that?"

"Well, I thought about it, but I didn't know exactly who you were in trouble with, if you know what I mean. I mean I didn't want to get the cops in on something you might not be too happy having them in on. After Abraham gave me the big story it was too late, *he* didn't want any cops in on it. He made me promise I wouldn't

206

call them until he made a getaway. But listen, don't worry, Pete will call them." She sounded unsure, and added, "I hope."

Baker's mind blossomed hopefully with visions of notes being opened in the knick of time by Mary's father. "To be opened in case of . . ." Mary would have written on the envelope and Pete, right on cue, would rip the flap and read all about it, including exact location, etc.

"Did you leave him a note?" he asked.

"A note? Listen, I had no time for that, the Double-crosser was breathing down my neck, afraid I was going to double-cross him! I only hope Pete thinks something happened to me and not that I ran off for a temporary snit. We had this argument about my going out and he might think I took off because of that."

Of course, no notes or anything. What did he expect? That life was like soap operas?

"Hey," he said, refusing to lose the faith. "What did Abraham the Double-crosser tell you? Did he say why they grabbed me?"

"To kidnap you."

"Oh thanks, that's a big help to know that."

"For ransom."

"Nothing else? Not why? We don't have any money, at least I don't think so. Why me? I'm not famous, my mother isn't famous . . ." Was she? Did they kidnap soap opera actresses? Did they think she must be rich?

"He wouldn't tell me the whole story," Mary said.

"Frankly, I don't think he knows the whole story, if you want my opinion. He was scared because he didn't know he was getting mixed up in a kidnapping when he got involved with those two creeps downstairs. He and a couple of other guys were working for them. But I don't know what for."

Baker wasn't really listening anymore. It was no use, she wasn't going to be any help at all. They wanted bodies, bodies to use when they turned into men. And women, now that Mary was here.

"What's the matter?" she asked. "Why do you look so funny?"

"How can you see if I look funny or not?"

"Well, I can feel you look funny. I have very good intuition, I get vibrations."

"Well, how about vibrating us out of here?" Baker snapped. "You didn't accomplish much, did you, with all your intuition? We're stuck here in this attic, waiting to be killed, and we don't even know where we are."

"Oh, I know where we are," Mary said. Her glasses glinted at him, catching a fine thread of light from one of the holes in the roof, making her look enigmatic, mysterious.

"Where?"

"In Maine. Place called Sawtruck, I think, at least it's near Sawtruck Centre. I saw the sign."

When Baker said nothing in return, she leaned forward to peer at him, trying to see his face in the dark. "Well, what's wrong now?"

"Nothing, nothing," Baker mumbled. He was feeling hot and cold at the same time.

"Well, if you won't confide in me," Mary said, "I can't help you, can I?"

"Shut up," Baker whispered. "Just shut up."

Things were churning inside his brain. Gorshin lived in Sawtruck. Was there some connection? Don't be a schmuck, of course there was a connection, but why, how? For a mind-screeching, slow lost minute, he considered the possibility that Gorshin had kidnapped him. And he realized that this was no superfluous thought, that somewhere, buried deep, there was a reason for such a possibility. Something about Gorshin, from long ago. The thought lasted a few seconds longer and then slid, tantalizingly, out of reach. He heard a long, juicy sniff next to his ear.

"Hey," he said, "what are you doing? Crying?"

"Like hell," Mary said. But she sniffed again. "I'm getting hayfever from the dust up here."

"Listen, I'm sorry," Baker said. "A lot has been happening to my head lately, my mind has been getting blown. I think I'm going to crack up or something. Maybe I'm going crazy."

Mary was silent for a moment. Then she said, gingerly, "Do you want to talk about it?"

"Yeah." He laughed. "This is something, isn't it? Here we are, alone in the dark and our hands are tied."

"Well, we still have our mouths," Mary said, but added hastily, "I didn't mean it that way."

"Okay," Baker said, opening his mouth to start talking. He waited.

"I don't know what to say," he told her. "I don't know where you start with a thing like this."

"I'm not going to say something corny like 'at the beginning.' A lot of times you don't know where the beginning is, do you? You don't even know when your eyes just started looking out of your head and seeing things different." Mary's voice came softly out of the dark. The pressure of her shoulder against his was warm, understanding. He felt safe about talking, maybe because he couldn't see her in the dark.

"I guess maybe it was the garlic," he said. "Before that, I never really took any steps. I felt it was real, but I didn't do anything real about it. First it was closets, I used to be afraid of them. My mother would hold my hand and show me there was nothing in the closet. But when she went away and left me in my bed, I knew they came back again. I knew they were inside the closet.

"Then it spread to other things. The hallways, the bathroom, behind the living room curtains. They never made a move, they only watched me. I knew I had to do something to get them out of my house, to keep them on the outside. I don't know how I found out about the garlic. Maybe I got the idea reading *Dracula* or something. But it worked. They stayed outside, they didn't get in the house anymore. But I always had to be on my guard because they were constantly watching me. I knew they had a big nest somewhere and I tried to find it. And after a while, I got to know that they were dangerous, not only to me but to the entire earth. It all came to me and it seemed true. That's why I think I'm going crazy. Because all of a sudden the whole idea seems nuts. And if the idea is nuts, then I must be a nut for thinking it up."

"Who are 'they'?" Mary asked quietly.

"The Slynacks. Gurngy gushes from outer space, strinny gringles, creatures who can change their shape, who slish through the smallest crack, who can kill you, absorb you, change into you. That's how I used to describe them. I used to be afraid to walk down the stairs in my building. I used to be able to smell them in the halls. I knew they followed me everywhere. I thought they were the ones who kidnapped me. Now I'm not so sure."

He turned toward her. "So what do you think of that? Real crackers, huh? I always knew nobody would believe me. They'd think I was bananas. Even I think I'm bananas, but I can't help having this terrible feeling, what if I'm right? What if it is true?"

"Listen, anything's possible," Mary said. "I really mean that. I have this old book from when I was a kid and it talks about the moon like some place no one was ever going to get to. But I have one question. Did these Slynacks ever actually attack you? Did they ever hurt you or anybody else?"

"You don't have to humor me, you know."

"I'm not humoring you, I'm serious, did they ever do anything to you in any way?"

"No."

"That's very interesting," Mary said. She seemed to be mumbling to herself.

"Okay, why is it interesting?" Baker asked.

"Because you saw them only as a threat. That's fairly typical, you know. People are afraid of what they don't understand. They feel threatened so they talk themselves into believing the danger is real. I wouldn't want to bet on the chances for any intergalactic visitors to this planet. The army would probably drop an H-bomb on them just to be on the safe side."

"I don't see your point."

"What I mean is, why do you believe the Slynacks are bad? Why not believe they're good, or at the very least neutral? Assuming you actually did make contact with some alien form of life, and allowing for the fact that they never actually harmed you in any way, why not change your opinion of them? You might find it very enlightening. You only get back what you give out in life. The same probably applies to Slynacks."

Although Baker made a series of deprecating and disbelieving noises, he was stunned. And he felt foolish, sort of embarrassed. Assuming, as Mary said, that Slynacks did exist, could he have made a terrible mistake?

"Like a bunch of guardian angels," he said to her. "I don't buy that."

"Listen, where do you think guardian angels came from? Why do you think people have such ideas? All myths are based in reality. We probably came from another planet ourselves. Otherwise we wouldn't have this obsession about heaven being up there in the sky."

While Baker was trying to find some non-saccharine way to tell Mary he was grateful for her help, there was a thudding from outside the attic. The unmistakable sound of boxes being moved, and the door opened to reveal Farn.

"Hi there," Mary said brazenly. "You're just in time. I want to go to the ladies' room."

"I thought I heard noise," Farn said. "What's going on?"

"Bathroom, toilet, lavatory, john, pee-pee, wee-wee?"

"No dirty talk," Farn reprimanded. "You can use the can, but I'll have to tape you up."

"I'm not using any can."

Farn looked blank. Slowly it dawned on him that Mary was going to present him with a new set of problems. "I'm taping both of you up," he snarled. "Then I'll take you to the privy."

He didn't know what Grepp would say about his taking the girl outside the house. But when he had taped her mouth up good and prodded her down the stairs, he was relieved to see that Grepp was still in conference with Abraham. "Make it snappy now," he told her and they ran down the narrow path to the outhouse, clothes

213

and skin catching on the brambles drooping at either side. He waited outside, holding the door shut. He was nervous because he had to untie her hands.

"Don't make it a habit," he told her when he had her safely back upstairs. He pushed her into the attic space, made sure the two of them were tied securely. "I don't like to do it, you know," he said in a friendly way. He knew they didn't believe him, but it was true. If he could, he would try to bring some extras for breakfast. The girl looked like she had a big appetite. He covered the hole, pushed the boxes into place and slammed the closet door shut.

In the dark, Mary and Baker looked at each other, but there was nothing to see.

None of them knew that down in the tunnel, beneath the cottage floor, Gorshin was making his way back to his house, an idea growing at the back of his mind.

24

On West 10th Street in New York City, Mrs. Clare Dilloway sat near the telephone, which was now surrounded by recording equipment, ashtrays overflowing with cigarette butts, empty paper cups and the remains of three pastrami sandwiches. When Katz was not waiting with her, one or two of his other men were, lounging on the couch or sprawled on the floor, reading her paperbacks and drinking endless cups of coffee. The phone did not ring. Half-asleep in the chair, she kept reminding herself that she had to call in sick in the morning. They would have to write her out of the show for a few days. Have her get hit by a truck or something nice like that. They could even get her kidnapped.

A few blocks east, on MacDougal Street, Pete told Sondra he wasn't coming up to her apartment that night. He was going to the local precinct to talk to a detective he knew. Mary was among the missing. "I'm gonna do better by that kid," he told Sondra, "try to be more understanding." But when Sondra warmed to the subject of Pete's relationship with his daughter, he cut her off by saying, "It's none of your business, she's my kid."

Sondra hung up on him. Slamming the receiver down, Pete turned to one of his waiters and said, "Wait till I get my hands on her, I'll kill her." The waiter shrugged, he was used to his boss' kooky daughter, and he didn't want to get involved in a family argument. That's why he didn't tell Pete that his daughter had gone off with the weirdo in the overcoat. The guy was too old for Mary, Pete wouldn't like it and he'd end up taking it out on him. Better to do himself a favor and keep quiet so he could keep his job.

Up in Sawtruck, Maine, Doc Pepper washed up the dirty coffee cups and emptied the garbage so his wife wouldn't have to face a mess first thing in the morning. He had sent John Bones home to bed, telling him to sleep tight and stop worrying about it. Good advice which he couldn't take himself. But who would have expected anything to happen after all these years? It had been Doc's personal opinion they were wasting their time on such a stale case and that's why he tired to encourage Gorshin to go back home. They had done Gorshin and his family an injustice, keeping up the subterfuge, and many's the time he wanted to tell George he knew.

Yawning and stretching, Doc looked like he was ready for a nice relaxed sleep, but inside his mind was still working hard. It might not be a bad idea to get a search warrant and see what was doing in the old house next to Gorshin's farm. Doc chuckled. He wouldn't mind getting a few leads, even breaking the case himself. Show the Feds a thing or two, show them they weren't hicks up here in Maine.

Also in Sawtruck, George Gorshin was busy resurrecting a carefully buried lead box. Inside it were ten thin vials, cradled in Styrofoam. He removed one of them, just enough for a Zinger and a Zapper. His plan was simple. He was going to knock on the door of the house next door and tell them he was ready to make a deal. Then he would have to find a way to slip a Zinger into a drink or a cup of coffee. He was going to do the same dirty rotten thing they had wanted to do, intrude on the ultimate privacy of an unsuspecting mind. Except in this case he had no compunctions about it, and it was the only way to find out what he wanted to know. Who killed Petersen, who killed Felix, who was behind the whole operation. If he could get these facts by asking a few well-placed questions that might not be answered verbally but which surely would stimulate some informative thoughts that could be read, he would turn the whole thing over to Doc Pepper. Doc would enjoy having a nice meaty situation like this dumped in his lap, he had always wanted to sink his teeth into something more substantial than traffic violations.

Gorshin didn't think he would have too much trouble getting out of the house once he found out what he wanted to know. If they made a deal they would have to let him go and get the drug. And instead of getting it, he would be phoning Doc. They wouldn't know he'd read their minds and they wouldn't know it was going to be the last reading for everybody. Because he was going to do something he should have done long ago.

He picked up the remaining nine vials, all that was left of his discovery. Once destroyed, there was no proof they had ever existed. He wasn't sure he could repeat the formula without his notes, and they were nothing more than some black ashes on the hillside. He certainly wasn't going to try. As far as the world was concerned, he didn't know a damn thing about reading minds. He would tell Doc they had been after the usual stuff, dope.

Doc was in for a big surprise.

What would have surprised Gorshin was that Felix Forbisher was very much alive. And for the second time in his life, terrified and running to the cops.

25

It was cozy being together under the eaves. Except for the fact that his tailbone was mortified, Baker felt happier than he had felt in a long time, perhaps his whole life. It was like some burden had been lifted. He was sorry that Farn had taped their mouths up again; he wanted to talk to Mary some more, tell her about his father dying and ask her about herself. It was funny the way things happened in life. If he hadn't been kidnapped, he would never have known what she was really like. He would have kept on being prejudiced, thinking of her as fat and weird and probably boring. He promised himself never to judge by appearance again.

It wasn't all roses, though; he was scared. Kept getting flashes of doom, and he felt cheated. He had a lot of things to do in the world, like make it up with the Slynacks, for instance. Because as Mary said, anything's possible, isn't it? It gave him a whole new outlook on life, he was looking forward to not having to run up and down the fire escape and worry about Slynack fortifications all the time. Also, he felt sorry for his mother. She was always so worried about him, locking the locks and walking him down the stairs. He could

219

imagine how she felt now, thinking he had been mugged, beaten up, hacked to death at last. She would go to the police right away, but how would they ever find him in Sawtruck? Nobody would think of looking for him here.

Eventually, he fell asleep, his head against Mary's well-padded shoulder. It was an uneasy sleep because of the tape on his mouth. He kept dreaming he was suffocating.

Next to him, Mary was wiggling her toes on the foot without the boot, trying to keep the circulation going. You think they would have given her boot back when she asked, her damn foot was freezing. She wasn't giving up, however, not a chance. Those schlumps downstairs weren't getting the better of her and besides, she had to save Baker. He needed protecting. She didn't know how he had managed to survive in New York for so long. Once his mind was straightened out and he got rid of some of his obsessions, he could turn out to be fairly interesting. They could be friends, who knows, even lovers. The first guy she met who wasn't on the make and they had to be tied up. And even worse, gagged so they couldn't talk. She could already be helping him clear out the dregs in his brain. If they got out of this, they would see a lot of each other, spend a lot of time rapping, and she could give up the tail scene. As Pete said, she was good psychoanalyzing everybody else, maybe she didn't spend enough time finding out about herself. Maybe all she had been looking for was some One. Listen, why kid herself, she knew damn well that was what she had been looking for. It could be that she had found him, but it was still touch and go as far as his feelings were concerned. They were sort of soul mates now, having been through this mess together. But you couldn't tell about people. Sometimes when they shared some big trauma with you, they wanted to get rid of you afterward. Because you kept reminding them of what happened. She hoped it wouldn't be that way with Baker. She wasn't going to let him off the hook that easily.

Downstairs, Farn was having one of his attacks of conscience. Should he tell Grepp about the gags? About the girl having to go outside to use the privy? He didn't care as much for the two of them as he did for the dog. Maybe if he stirred Grepp up about the boy and girl he would forget the dog and giving it the nice painless death and not see the chewed rope. Farn was thinking of taking the dog back home with him. A dog would be a nice innovation. Nobody had dogs at home. He decided to tell Grepp.

Grepp was distracted. He was thinking about phone calls. The situation was ridiculous. A kidnapping and now nothing. The fact that he could now barter two for the price of one was not cheering. He didn't even know who the girl was. She called herself Mary the Hulk and he felt this was some kind of made-up name, an alias. He was afraid she would be tough as nails under interrogation, confessing only her social security number. He was aware that Farn was moaning in his ear. "What?" he asked.

Farn broke the news and got his planned results. Grepp immediately went into action. He seemed to have completely forgotten about the dog.

Brutally, Baker was awakened from his fitful sleep. Grepp kicked him aside as he and Farn dragged Mary's unwilling body from the attic. Baker heard the thumps and bumps as they took Mary away. The hole was closed up again and he was left in an excruciating position which seemed impossible to get out of. He was hit by an attack of anxiety tremens, long overdue. He started to shake and then choke. His tongue didn't seem to have enough room anymore and was convulsively trying to jerk itself down his throat. One of the rubber bands had come off his teeth and was crawling around inside his mouth like a worm. He tried to get a hold on himself, talk himself out of it. He was not choking, his heart was not twanging like a bedspring, he was not going to die. I'm too young to have a heart attack, he told himself. After all, I am Immute and Behooveless. His lymphocytic macrophages were still multiplying. Come on, nothing could harm him. He was Baker D., survivor of nurnburn. Mr. Big.

His boys would be here soon, armed with two sub-machine guns and a bazooka. They would take the house as easy as spit, he and Mary would drive back to town in the Cadillac, drinking martinis, cool white ones straight up with a lemon twist (the Caddy had a built-in bar). He could see Mary languishing against the leopard-patterned seats (fake fur, he was no ecological moron), wearing a satin gown cut low in the chest. Platinum hair (she had a quick rinse) cascaded around her pink shoulders. The boys never failed Mr. Big. They'd be here any minute now.

And furthermore, there were Slynacks on his side now, spreading their gursy schlucks around the house, ready to gringe in through the slits in the roof and save Baker from the jaws of Grepp.

He felt better. His heart stopped twanging. The rubber band slipped down into the side of his jaw and stayed still, no longer a worm.

Slowly, the dawn seeped through the holes in the roof. Another day was coming. There was no way to tell if Slynacks came along with it.

Grepp heard the knock, but he couldn't believe his ears. His first thought was Farn, bumping into things as usual. But Farn himself came running.

"Someone's at the door, Grepp!"

"Control yourself, Farn," Grepp said. "There's nothing to worry about. Tell Abraham to go down in the tunnel. You get fixed up, but don't use so much lipstick this time. It's only seven A.M."

Farn scuttled away to put on his long dressing gown and get into bed like Grepp's invalid wife. Grepp took a deep breath, not as calm as he wanted Farn to believe, and opened the door. He didn't have to put on any acts to look disgruntled and sleepy. Fully expecting to see the fat policeman, he was appalled when he found Gorshin.

"Good morning," Gorshin said. Grepp gaped. With difficulty he gathered his wits enough to say, "Yes, what is it?" as if he had no idea who the man was.

"I'm your neighbor, George Gorshin. But I'm sure you already know that. I think we have some talking to do. Can I come in?"

"Talk about what?" Grepp asked, doggedly keeping up the act. "My wife is ill, it's very early."

"Sorry about your wife, that's too bad. How is your dog, by the way? He looked a little thin when I saw him last. A little hungry, too."

"Come in," Grepp said, "come in."

"Thanks," Gorshin said. He heard the door being bolted behind him. He walked directly into the main room of the house, noticing the windows were heavily draped. There was a pervading smell of mildew. The room held a couple of armchairs and a table. Junk piled in the corner. He sat down in one of the chairs. Grepp stood behind him.

224

"What can I do for you?" he asked amiably.

"I'm not going to beat around the bush," Gorshin said. "I came to make a deal."

Wary of tricks, Grepp played dumb. "What kind of deal?"

"You know what kind. The same one you made to me twelve years ago. Only this time, the price is higher."

"Inflation, no doubt," Grepp said. "What are we selling?"

"I'm selling, you're buying."

"It appears you've changed your mind, Mr. Gorshin. Why?"

"I'm tired. Simple as that."

Grepp was confused. It should have been the other way around, Gorshin buying his son for the price of the drug. "Are you sure it's so simple?" he asked.

"Sure. I sell out, you stop hounding me, everybody gets what he wants, everybody's happy."

But no mention of his son. "Well, well," Grepp said. He stood at the side of Gorshin's chair. "Please make no sudden moves," he said. "Stand up and take off your jacket."

Gorshin, his face showing traces of amusement, took the jacket off and threw it aside, well out of reach. He held up his trouser legs so that Grepp could see he was clean. "I'm not armed," he said, turning.

"I am," Grepp said and Gorshin found himself looking down the barrel of an ugly weapon.

225

"Please sit down again," Grepp requested and he took the other chair opposite Gorshin, thinking Where is that fool, Farn? Surely he can hear what's going on.

"You don't have to keep that thing pointed at me," Gorshin said. "I came here to cooperate fully, believe me. I'm ready to make a deal, I told you that."

"This sudden change of heart," said Grepp, "it makes me uneasy."

"Look," Gorshin explained. "I'm tired of having you and whoever else is behind you on my tail. I want some peace and quiet. I've been running for almost twelve years; ten of them up here, and I thought I was safe, but now I see it's impossible to be safe anymore. I'm finished running."

"That's the only reason, you're tired of running away? No other reason for suddenly wanting to cooperate?"

Gorshin looked at him. "What other reason should there be? Isn't that enough?" He thought for a moment. "If you mean money, sure, I need the money."

Was it possible the man really knew nothing about his son? Grepp heard Farn creeping down the stairs. He hoped he had taken off the gown and the makeup, but you couldn't be sure with Farn.

"We might be able to work something out," Grepp said.

Gorshin put his head in his hands, looking like a man at the end of his strength. "Could I have some coffee?" he asked. "I'm just about beat."

Grepp seized on this suggestion. A good way to keep

226

Farn from coming in the room. If Gorshin was in the dark about his son, he didn't want Farn walking in making allusions and suggestions. "Make us some coffee," he yelled out to the hallway. "But stay in the kitchen. Let me know when it's ready."

As they listened to Farn smashing things in the kitchen, Grepp pondered this amazing new development. Here, right in front of him, was the goods they had been after, the man actually offering to sell his precious secret for reading minds. Not that Grepp actually believed Gorshin had such a thing, but it was Grepp's job to get whatever the stuff was and find out. The Top thought Grepp was doing the job purely for financial gain and Grepp let him think it. Avarice was a typical human failing. The Top was planning to sell the drug to others for a big profit. But money held no interest for Grepp. He had other reasons for wanting to get his hands on the drug. Reasons the Top knew nothing about.

Farn called from the kitchen. "Put it down in the hall," Grepp said, "and go ustairs. You might want to check on a couple of things." Farn did as he was told, but he was annoyed. When was he supposed to feed the prisoners? There wouldn't be much left to bargain with if they didn't keep them alive.

When Farn was out of the way again, Grepp directed Gorshin to get the tray of coffee from the hall. Gorshin was almost afraid to trust his luck. The coffee had been easy, too easy. Now all he had to do was put an equal

227

amount of the drug into both cups. That way, there would be no problem about who took which cup and Gorshin could add the rest of the vial to his own cup so that he received the larger dosage. It sounded simple. It had to be. On the way to the hall he slid the vial out of his pocket. It was wrapped in a crumpled handkerchief and he stopped to blow his nose. "Sorry," he said. "I have sinus trouble." He vigorously wiped his nostrils, managing to open the vial.

Grepp was not interested in Gorshin's sinuses and was not really worried about him. If anything, he was worried about who might be waiting outside, but he felt things were reasonably safe while Gorshin remained in plain view, unable to give signals. He would set up the deal and make arrangements to get the drug which Gorshin obviously hadn't been stupid enough to bring along. If there was any funny business, he would play his trump card and hold the boy as hostage until Gorshin delivered the goods. He paid no attention to which cup Gorshin took from the tray, but as soon as Gorshin was seated he said, "I'll take your cup, if you don't mind, and you can have mine," just in case Gorshin had slipped in a mickey to put Grepp out of commission. Gorshin changed cups willingly and then got his handkerchief out again and hacked up some phlegm. "Damn nuisance," he said to Grepp, "I must be getting a cold."

But he had overplayed it. Grepp cried, "What are you doing?" and it was all over. Gorshin tried to dump the coffee, but he stopped in the face of the gun. "Hold it,"

Grepp snarled and took the cup away, putting it up on the mantel over the fireplace. Grepp's cup, containing the Zinger dose was left on the table next to Grepp's chair.

"What were you trying to do? Poison yourself?" he asked, and when Gorshin gave no answer, "I don't think so. All this talk about making a deal was nothing but lies. You didn't come here to make a deal." Gorshin remained silent. He was worried about the two cups of coffee, hoping Grepp wouldn't suspect what they contained and, if he did, know about the proportionate dosage. Still, he had made a bad blunder. All they had to do now was analyze the coffee and they'd be halfway there.

"Farn," Grepp yelled and Farn came running. "Take Mr. Gorshin into the other room and see that he's restrained. But don't bother to restrain his mouth. We have something to discuss."

"You don't understand . . ." Gorshin tried to say, but Farn was pressing a place on his neck. His legs suddenly felt like water and his head started to buzz. "Gently now, Farn," Gorshin heard Grepp say, and he found himself stumbling out of the room, black specks getting in the way of his eyes.

Grepp stayed in the living room, contemplating the cup on the mantel. A lot of ideas were fighting for precedence in his mind. He didn't think Gorshin was trying to poison himself, no point in that. Most likely the cup contained the drug for reading minds. So, it seemed as if it was possible that Gorshin had made such a discovery after all, and had planned to use it on them while he pretended to negotiate a deal. Having the drug in the coffee was as good as having it signed, sealed and delivered to the Top. The Top would have the coffee analyzed and Grepp would be paid for a job well done. But since Grepp never had any real intentions of turning anything over to the Top, he picked up the cup and swallowed its contents without regret.

He went into the room where Gorshin was now tied to a chair, looking dazed and weak, but recovered from Farn's manipulations.

"All right, Farn," he said. "You can go now." He felt very excited. His heart was beating fast and he was perspiring.

"What did you do with the coffee?" Gorshin asked.

"I threw it away," Grepp said. "I don't like monkey business."

Gorshin took a deep breath of relief. The other cup of coffee, Grepp's cup with the Zinger, wouldn't do any harm. It wouldn't matter who drank it. It was plainly a case of overestimation on his part, these people didn't know what they were doing.

Farn, irked at being preemptorily dismissed, wandered into the living room, vaguely thinking of cleaning up. He saw the coffee on the table. It looked untouched.

I'll give it to the boy, he thought. There was no

sense wasting it. They were very low on coffee and low on water too. If they didn't get out of here soon they were all going to starve now that Klinc wasn't around to do the shopping and Grepp wouldn't let either one of them be seen in the village.

Farn would have drunk it himself, naturally, but he already had a cup in the kitchen and too much coffee gave him heartburn. The boy could use a stimulant, something to pick him up after being kicked in the stomach by Grepp.

"I brought you a surprise," he said to Baker, who didn't seem in much of a mood for surprises. He removed the tape from the boy's mouth.

When Baker saw the surprise was a cup of black coffee he wanted to throw up. Just what he didn't need, but he supposed it would get rid of the slimy feeling in his mouth. He worked his tongue for a moment and spat out the rubber band. Farn held the cup to his lips.

"Thanks," he said before he drank.

"You're welcome," Farn said, feeling pleased. What Grepp doesn't know won't hurt him, he thought.

"What did you do with Mary?" Baker asked after he had swished the last of the murky liquid around in his mouth. Now that it was gone, he wished he had some more.

"Nothing."

"Come on, what do you mean nothing? Where did you put her?"

231

"In the linen closet." Farn didn't want to talk about her. Of all of them including the dog, he liked her least of all.

"You bastards," Baker said.

Farn was insulted. He put the tape back on and didn't bother to put Baker in a more comfortable position, even though he could see his legs were bent the wrong way.

Baker was left alone again. Squelching the panic that never seemed to go away, he limped his way back into dreams.

26

"Why did you come here?" Grepp asked Gorshin. "What's the real reason?"

"I told you, to make a deal," Gorshin replied.

Grepp was beginning to get waves in his head, he was hearing voices, and he prepared himself to begin reading Gorshin's mind.

Up in the attic, the Zinger was spreading through Baker's system. He wasn't aware of it, he felt too lousy to notice any new symptoms. He was busy concentrating on being Immute and Behooveless, the only thing he had ever done to exercise his insecure brain. *The boys will be coming all right*, he dreamed, *led by the Stump (receding hairline, nervous eyes missing nothing, a big rod in a shoulder holster, another one in his hand). The Stump never let him down, he could always count on the Stump, he was one of his best men.*

"Is the Stump your boss?" Grepp asked Gorshin.

"My Boss? What are you talking about?"

Grepp smiled. He could lie all he wanted to, Grepp knew what was going on inside.

233

It wouldn't take them long to get here, they knew where he was, Sawtruck, Maine, blow the place right off the map.

"Does anyone know you're here?"

"I live here, remember?" Gorshin said. But Grepp knew better than to believe him.

I'm hungry, Baker thought, guts sloshing around, cramps. I wonder what he was doing with blood all over his lips that time. Dracula coming in the window, big teeth hanging out. Smiling, eyebrows in his hair, leaning over the white neck of his victim, sssslllup, drinking blood. Crawling down the side of the castle like a big bug (saw that in a movie once, scared the shit out of me). Not scared anymore. The boys are coming to get me. Come out with your hands up (sound of machine-gun fire)! Throwing tear gas and Mace. Big boots stomping up the stairs. Clunk thud! Ack Ackackackackackack (more machine-gun fire).

Grepp was mildly disconcerted. "Why don't you tell me the truth, Mr. Gorshin?"

"I told you the truth, you don't believe me," Gorshin said. He looked at Grepp, wondering why there were such long silences in between questions. Grepp seemed to be concentrating on something beyond the room.

I wonder what happened to Red, is she still waiting? Better forget Red, she's in the past, like the Slynacks.

234

No wait, Slynacks still here, Mary said so, good guys now. Leap higher than tall buildings (vision of a Slynack stretching itself into the sky, higher than the Empire State Building, long and green, full of warts, bumpy lumpy with big pointed teeth, no, that's vampires). Slynacks can get in anywhere. Go all stringy and come through the keyhole, they'll wind themselves around Farn and Grepp like green spaghetti, glishing, syrupy Slynacks, squeezing tighter and tighter.

Gorshin noticed that Grepp looked frightened.

It's time to attack. Get them Slynacks! Sic 'em, you space blisters.
   The boys are coming too. It's all right, they have the house surrounded. They have guns, grenades, they're going to blow this place up. He could see them, a vast army approaching, led by the Stump and the boys, followed by Slynacks, and coming up behind, last of all, the vampires, gnashing and gnawing acicular teeth, grinning in the sun.

To Gorshin's surprise, Grepp suddenly rushed out of the room.

"Pack up," he said to Farn. "We're clearing out of here."
   "What? Who?" Farn asked.
   "On second thought, never mind the packing."
   "I don't get it," said Farn.

Grepp didn't get it either, but he wasn't waiting around to find out. Gorshin had definitely discovered a mind-reading drug, and in the event of such a possibility, Grepp had planned to get the drug away from him, to take such a dangerous thing out of everybody's hands. But he was no hero. He was no match for an army, especially the kind of army that was coming here. As far as the Top was concerned, Grepp had no qualms. He had never intended to give him the means to read minds. Normally, he would prefer clearing out in a more honorable way, telling the Top that Gorshin's discovery was nothing more than common everyday LSD. But now the Top would have to take care of himself. Grepp wasn't waiting around for grenades and machine guns and monsters with sharp teeth.

He hurried Farn out of the house, remembered Abraham and hurried back in. When they looked in the tunnel, Abraham was nowhere to be found. "I'm not surprised," Grepp said and slammed the door down on the dog who was looking up expectantly, wagging his tail.

"About the dog, Grepp," Farn started to say, but Grepp threw him into the car.

"I don't understand you," Farn said, his head hitting the roof of the Volkswagen as they bounced over the ruts, "why leave them all there? Why?"

"You have a better suggestion, I suppose?"

"Sure. I thought you wanted to kill them."

"What did I tell you from the very beginning, Farn? That nobody would get hurt."

"I know that," Farn whined. "But you took it so seriously. I thought you wanted to play the part right, all the way to the end."

"Don't you think we did it right?" Grepp asked, forgetting the brakes as they took a curve. "You don't think we acted like authentic gangsters?"

"You should know," Farn said, hanging on for his life. "You're the one who read all the books to find out how to act."

"Well, it's over now," Grepp said. "It doesn't matter now."

"Still . . ." Farn said as they pulled up a lonely cowpath and Grepp stopped the car.

"Still what?"

"They can talk."

"And what are they going to say?" Grepp took hold of the loose flesh below his chin and pulled. The rubber came away from his face, taking his features and the wig of white hair with it. Farn ruminated awhile, thinking about the dog. Then he did the same thing.

"This is where we get off," Grepp said.

"I know. And you can stop giving me orders. I don't work for you anymore."

"Thank you anyway," Grepp said. "For your help."

"You didn't accomplish much," was Farn's retort. Grepp was silent. What could he say? That he had set out to save the world? Perhaps Gorshin would be sensible and get rid of his dangerous drugs.

In a few moments the Volkswagen was empty, its occupants gone. A breeze rippled along the empty cowpath. There was no one there.

27

It was Charlie who found them. Gorshin, having cut his hands free by rubbing the rope back and forth on one of the many rusty nails protruding from the walls, had left the house with only one intention: get in touch with Doc Pepper. Surprisingly enough, he met Doc himself coming up the road to the house with John Bones at the wheel of the car, wincing at every jolt.

"Here now, George," Doc said, waving a piece of paper in front of his nose, "what's going on here? We have a search warrant."

"Nothing to search," Gorshin told him. "They're gone."

Charlie, who had balked at leaving the house with Gorshin, now took the opportunity to run back inside.

"He was kidnapped," Gorshin said to Doc. "Guess he doesn't know what he's doing, poor old hound."

"George," Doc said, looking very serious. "There's something I want to tell you. You may not be aware . . ." At that moment Charlie set up his own special brand of howl.

Gorshin dropped Doc in midstream and ran back. Poor Charlie had flipped out, the strain on his nerves

239

had been too much for him. Doc puffed his way after Gorshin, and Bones sprinted past. They found Charlie upstairs, scratching furiously at a closet door, his howls cracking into frantic barks. They looked at each other and then Doc came forward and opened the door. "Nothing but a lot of junk in here."

But Charlie was snuffling down behind a pile of boxes now, showing them another door. It was a shock to open it up and find a body. Even more of a shock to pull it out and see who it was.

Baker was not shocked. "They kidnapped me," he said, and when he tried to stand up he fell down again.

"Take it easy, your legs are numb. Who kidnapped you?"

"I don't know. How did you and Charlie find me?"

Gorshin started to tell him and then stopped. "Never mind that right now," he said. "Clare must be out of her mind."

They started to help him downstairs. "Hey, wait a minute," Baker said. "There's somebody else."

"What?"

"A friend of mine. She tried to rescue me." He looked proud. "She's in the linen closet, unless they bumped her off."

Gorshin could only croak. They found Mary under the bottom shelf of the linen closet. The door had been padlocked and it took some time getting it open. It was a tight squeeze. It took Mary a while to unbend.

Doc waited around long enough to get Mary's name and address in full and then he and Bones went back to the car. There was a certain new bounce to Doc's walk and he looked positively gleeful. He couldn't wait to give the Feds the news. As they went out the door, he and Bones were slapping each other on the back.

"If you two can make it to my house," Gorshin said to Baker and Mary, "you can collapse there. Food and beds is what you need and I have all the comforts of home.

"Practically all," he added. "Some of it is in a parking lot somewhere."

They were going out the front door when Gorshin stopped and said, "I'll show you something," and took them to the tunnel. "They dug it out," he explained, "from here over to my cellar. Amazing."

Baker's face turned greener than it already was.

"What's the matter?" Mary asked. "Going to puke?"

"Slynacks," he whispered to her, "are a burrowing, tunneling people."

She raised her eyebrows.

They rode back to Gorshin's cellar on the Thumper. But of course none of them knew that was its name.

"Clare," Gorshin said, "are you okay? Somebody wants to talk to you." She had heard the news from Katz only moments before, but she was still afraid to believe it.

"I'm okay," Baker was saying, "I'm really fine. So

241

don't worry, okay? I'm putting Gorshin back on, he wants to speak to you."

Katz was running around waving his hands, giving signals she didn't understand. "George," she cried into the phone, "what the hell has been going on?"

Katz took the phone away from her. "Mr. Gorshin," he said, "I'm glad to hear your son is out of danger. Now, have they made any attempts to contact you? What's that? What?"

They were going to New York in the morning. Gorshin insisted they stay in Sawtruck for the night, overriding the wishes of Katz, Clare Dilloway and Mary's father, Pete. He made a fire and opened a couple of dozen of Mrs. Thwaite's bottles and jars to make them a meal. Then he told Doc they were incommunicado, no matter what happened.

The three of them didn't talk much. At least not about the ordeal. Gorshin told them to wait for the FBI to give them the facts, but he knew he was the one who was copping out. Baker was sitting on the floor next to the fire, staring at him. Was he finding similarities? Did he suspect what everybody else seemed to have known all along? If Baker asked, he'd have to say yes. But he wanted to talk to Clare first.

Baker didn't ask. He was in a pleasantly painful stupor. Pleasant because he was lying on two pillows with a full stomach and there was no more tape across his gringy mouth. Painful because his arms and legs were aching.

Mary was roasting her blue toes as close to the fire as possible. She had eaten like a horse, even worse than usual, but she didn't care. She must have lost twenty pounds in the linen closet in pure sweat alone.

After a while Gorshin left them together, saying he was going to bed. He had shown them where they could sleep, but he had a feeling they were going to stay in front of the fire all night, dozing and talking and savoring something between them that he couldn't be a part of.

"Goodnight," Mary said to him, "and hey, listen, thanks for getting me out of that closet."

"He's great," Mary said to Baker. "A sort of balding knight in shining armor who saved us in the knick of time. Talk about the movies."

"It's a good thing he did, I certainly wasn't capable of being much help."

"Oh, don't start egoizing at a time like this. How about me? Fat Sister to the rescue! I'd say we cancelled each other out."

Baker leaned upon an elbow. "What did you think about Farn and Grepp?"

"Half-assed. But I know what you mean. They'll probably get caught."

"Maybe." They were quiet for a while and then Mary came over closer and put her head on the pillow next to his.

"Here we are, alone at last," she said. "Guess what, without my glasses you look very ephemeral."

"If that's a come-on, I'm not up to it."

"Neither am I."

Baker laughed. "But it's our big chance, we should take advantage of it."

"You're forgetting the chaperone. I must say we've had a lot of chaperones lately."

"We'll have to wait until we're really alone." He didn't know if he wanted to kiss her yet. He felt too tired to put much into it anyway. But he moved his arm around her.

"Hey, are you a virgin?" she asked.

"I'm not telling."

"I know what that means but never mind, I'm not telling either, so we can both think we're not telling because of one reason when maybe the real reason isn't the reason at all." She stopped and took a deep breath. "You know what I just discovered? I talk too much, you were right."

"Me?"

"Yes, you told me I was a regular massacre. And I am."

She kept her trap shut after that. And they both fell asleep.

28

After it was all explained not everyone understood what
they had been told. And there were a couple of questions
that were never answered. The facts were that Felix
Forbisher had come out of hiding to set up his second
and almost as fatal deal, selling Gorshin's mind-reading
drug to the highest bidder. Calling himself by the code
name Top, he hired two people who fit the description
of Grepp and Farn to set up an operation right under
Gorshin's nose. Grepp then hired three small-time opera-
tors to help, namely Klinc, Boris and Abraham. All three
had been apprehended, but Grepp and Farn were still at
large. "We have the descriptions, but we can't get a
make on them," Katz said. "And they seemed to have
vanished from the face of the earth."

"How did Felix know I was still alive?" Gorshin wanted
to know, although he had a feeling it was a redundant
question.

"We offered Felix protection," Katz said. "In return
for information. He wasn't much help on the Petersen
case, but every now and then he would supply a few facts
about the activities of some of his buddies. Felix had a
long nose and a penchant for making deals. He gave out

245

a little and wanted a lot in return. A few well-placed questions in the right places and he sniffed out the fact that one George Gorshin might not be as dead as he pretended to be. Still hoping to make that big bundle, he cooked up a nice little deal for himself and got a nice advance on delivery. You know the outcome. He couldn't deliver the mind-reading drug any more than he could the first time. It was a mind-reading drug, wasn't it?"

"Mind reading?" Gorshin looked very surprised. "I never heard anything so ridiculous. I was developing a drug, yes, a hallucinogen. But mind reading?"

Katz chose not to pursue it. He was going to marry Gwen and they were blowing New York and taking off for points west. Gwen was delighted he wasn't a janitor anymore. Lil, unfortunately, didn't feel the same. "You can't keep help nowadays," she moaned. "They leave you in the lurch, every time."

"What's the story on the garlic?" he asked Baker before he left.

"Nothing," Baker said. "A dumb game I used to play. It's all over now."

Except for the missing Grepp and Farn, the loose ends had been tied into knots.

Gorshin was staying on 10th Street for a few days, but only a few, he had to get back to Charlie, who was boarding with Frank at the Country Store. He and Clare didn't have to break the news to Baker, he asked it himself almost right away.

246

"Mom," he said when Gorshin was taking a shower, "can I ask you a very important question and get a very straight answer?"

Clare Dilloway mashed her cigarette into the ashtray and immediately lit up another. As soon as all the excitement died down she was going to give up smoking. "What's the question?"

"No bullshit? You'll tell me the truth?"

She knew what was coming. It didn't surprise her when he asked, "Is Gorshin really my father?"

He thought he would feel elated, excited, like something great had happened, but when she said yes it was like something he had known all along. He felt good about it. Quietly. But he wondered what in hell was his last name. He asked her if she and Gorshin were going to get together again and she said, "It's been too long, this isn't a soap opera, Baker." But she cancelled her dates with Arnold. She told Baker he could go to Maine and stay with Gorshin for the next school holiday. Gorshin was planning to demolish the old house next to his farm, which he had made arrangements to buy. But he was keeping the tunnel. To remind him, he said. But he didn't say what.

He met Mary at the coffee house where they had first gone for cappuccino. "I'm not sentimental," Mary said, "but why not?" She was allowed out again after being kept in for a week by Pete, even though the police and Katz and his mother had explained everything.

247

"I've been doing a lot of thinking," Baker told her. "And I got it all figured out. You know how I told you about the Slynacks? Well, it was all a figment of my imagination. Like a substitution, you know? Maybe I remembered having Gorshin as my father and when he went away I had to find a reason. Like an excuse, because I couldn't let myself believe that my own father would desert me. So I invented the Slynacks. And I made them the ones who took my father away. Only it got a little out of hand, you know. Like I was getting really schizo."

Mary was laughing. "What's so damn funny?" he asked.

"I'm not laughing at you, I'm laughing at me. Pete's always saying I play psychiatrist too much. Well, you don't need my psychoanalysis, you've got it all figured out."

"Okay, so what do you think? Is it a good theory?"

"Sure it is," she said. She leaned toward him, pushing her rose-colored glasses up her nose. "But listen, don't forget what I told you. Anything's possible. Don't get too sane. It's bad for your health."

He was free, him, Baker D., free as a bird but not alone. It had been nice for a while, pretending Slynacks were friendly and helpful beings watching over him. Certainly a relief from the Slynack fortification days and the terrible smell of garlic. He could walk down the stairs now, open his window, stop looking over his shoulder for the

long green hand. But he didn't need the Slynacks anymore, bad or good.

It made him feel a little naked, stripped of all that
protection, a little vulnerable. But he had Mary and
Gorshin, better than any Slynacks, and he was ready to
take it as it came.

He felt good. Really really good!